Acoustics and Alibis

Dan DeKoning

DEDICATION

This book is dedicated to everyone who enjoys reading a good
mystery.

And to all the writers who create them.

Acoustics
and
Alibis

CHAPTER ONE

My name is Codi Lynn Cassidy. I'm really excellent at three things: writing and playing music, getting into trouble, and daydreaming. At the time, I found myself attracted to the third since I didn't have my guitar with me, and I didn't feel in the mood for trouble. So, I decided to daydream. I snapped out of my reverie and focused on the scenery passing by the window of the old bus. I took a moment to glance at the GPS on the dashboard. After getting both values, I compared its arrival time to the time on the radio display. Then I calculated I had forty-seven minutes, give or take until we arrived in Quincey, New Mexico.

I looked at the driver, a tall hunk of a man, who currently entertained himself by singing to the radio while keeping the bus between the white lines.

"You want me to drive?" I asked.

He looked over at me and shook his head. "How many times have we had this discussion? There's no way you could handle this machine."

"I had to ask. You good for the next hour? If you need to pull over and take a rest, go ahead. We don't need to be there until this evening," I said.

Bozeman James dismissed me with a wave of his hand and turned his attention back to the road and the radio.

He was right, though. I couldn't drive the big bus. It was over thirty feet long and handled like a brick on wheels. Since I only stand two inches under five feet and can't tip the scale over one hundred pounds wearing my heaviest boots, it's not designed to be driven by a waif like me. I bought it from a retired musician who moved into a retirement community. Although I really didn't need something so large, since he was a good friend of my mom's, he made me an offer I truly couldn't refuse. I admit, there were times I regretted buying the rolling fortress, but those times were far and few between. Bozeman is a skilled tinkerer who keeps the old bus rolling with equal parts mechanical know-how, duct tape, and magic. We have an equal partnership, and we split the bus duties fifty-fifty. Bozeman drives the bus and handles the maintenance, and I keep it clean, and the tiny refrigerator and the adjoining pantry stocked. It's important that the bus feels like a home. We spend over three hundred days on the road, traveling from town to town, doing laps through every state west of the great plains. After all, I can't make a living as a roaming singer/songwriter and cowgirl poet if I don't roam.

Bozeman reached forward and turned the volume down on the radio. "You plan out the set list for tomorrow night?"

"Almost have it done. I need to talk to Sam before I firm it up. We'll see her tonight when we meet her for dinner. From what I gather, it'll be mostly covers, but I'm hoping to get a few originals in."

"How long we playing for? Our usual ninety minutes?"

"Need to shore that up, too. It's one of those gigs where we're playing a set through dinner, and we may do a separate set after dinner."

Bozeman shook his head. "C'mon, Codi, you know how I hate playing during dinner. People are more interested in those side conversations and eating than they are in paying any attention to us."

I understood exactly what Bozeman meant. A concert over dinner meant no attention paid to us, like we were nothing more than background noise. And usually, we got a cold plate of food ten minutes before the diners finished their meal. But it was a paying gig, and exposure, and if it's one thing I liked to do, it was getting good exposure. "I appreciate you hate them, and I normally wouldn't accept, but I'm doing it as a favor for a friend."

"Am I off track, or do you end up booking most of our gigs based on you doing favors for friends?" Bozeman asked.

I offered a smile as an answer, even though Bozeman didn't see my grin while he kept his eyes on the road. It was true. I booked a lot of shows based on leads from people in my circle, but that only accounted for just over fifty percent of the shows we did every year. The entertainment business was all about meeting people and collecting contacts and business cards, and you never knew who would be at a show. Lots of folks on the radio got there because they played a gig that some music producer or executive was at on happenstance.

"Hey, did I not get us at the Colorado State Fair last year? I didn't know anyone there," I said.

I glanced over and saw Bozeman trying to hide a smirk.

"Hey, I said most of the gigs, not all," Bozeman said. "I'm going to take a quick break after all. There's a wayside coming up."

A mile farther down the road, Bozeman pulled into a rest area and parked the bus between two idling semi-trucks.

"Are you getting out?" he asked as he unclasped his seatbelt and opened the door.

"I don't have to. I think I'll check on the kids."

Bozeman nodded, then disappeared through the door, and a glance through the window told me he needed to use the facilities in the worst way. Although we had a functioning bathroom on board, we visited public restrooms whenever possible, since Bozeman hated pumping out the gray water and black water tanks. I don't blame him for that, and every time it needs to be done, I suddenly have other important tasks I need to attend to.

I unbuckled, stepped into the kitchen, and rummaged around in a cabinet until I found the container of cat treats I wanted. Carefully, I shook three of the fish-shaped, salmon scented goodies into my palm, replaced the container, and started my search for Gibson.

Since we were on a bus, that meant limited places for Gibson to hang out. I looked around the small common area that contained the kitchen area. The area also held a small table, four chairs, and a built-in entertainment center that held a sound system and a television. Gibson was nowhere in sight. I walked down the hallway past the closed bathroom door, and the closed door to the room where we stored our performing gear. That left only two options.

I took a quick peek into Bozeman's room, and it took little effort to see Gibson wasn't in there, either. Bozeman is a tidy man, almost to the point of annoyance. He made up the twin bed with military precision. He squirreled away all his clothing in the small closest or compartments in his room. The small space smelled a bit like lemon, so I guessed he must have deep-cleaned recently, which he did once a week without fail. His room, like mine, had a small dressing table with a folding office chair, and his table held a few sheets of manuscript paper and a coffee mug filled with pens. I stepped over, glanced at the paper, read his scrawl, and determined he was writing a tune about some girl named Jenny. I continued on my quest to find the cat.

Way in the bus's rear was my bedroom. My bedroom, like Bozeman's, was spartan and held only a bed, table, and chair. Unlike Bozeman's room, mine looked a little more lived in. My bed had a bookshelf headboard stuffed with paperbacks, and although I pulled the bed's comforter up, the bed still looked messy. The foot of the bed held the two shirts I had tried on that morning before I settled on the T-shirt I currently had on. My desk held a couple more paperbacks, my laptop, and my favorite hairbrush. I owned a coffee mug that was a twin to Bozeman's. Instead of having only pens like his, mine held a single pen, hair ties, paper clips, pocket change, a butterscotch candy, guitar picks, and other assorted items. Around every six weeks, the mug fills up, then I'm forced to dump out the contents and clean it out. It's always a surprise to me what I find. I shouldn't have that mug at all since sometimes Merle or Dolly get in there, look for treasures, and spread the stuff all over the bus. On the bed were two pillows stacked one on top of the other, and on the top of the highest pillow slept Gibson, my cat. As I entered the room, Gibson opened one eye, stretched out a paw, then yawned while I approached. The five-year-old tuxedo cat sat up when I opened my hand and offered the treats to him. They were Gibson's favorite, so he ate them right out of my palm.

"Who's a good boy?" I picked up Gibson, put him over one shoulder like I was burping a baby, and scratched his ears and rubbed his back. In response, he nuzzled my ear and purred. I met Gibson at a gas station outside of Provo, Utah. When I headed to use the restroom, I heard a mewing coming from a cardboard box, and when I opened the box, there was Gibson with his big green eyes. He was only a couple months old then, was undernourished, and was the most pitiful creature I had ever seen. Of course, I fell in love with him right away and adopted him on the spot. The bus rocked, which meant that Bozeman had returned, so I gave Gibson a kiss on the forehead and placed him back on his pillow and returned to the passenger seat.

"How is everyone?" Bozeman asked as he strapped in and turned over the engine.

"You were back too soon, so I only found Gibson."

"I guessed that already," Bozeman said.

"How could you tell?"

"The black fur on your left ear."

Instinctively, I tugged at my ear, then looked in my hand.

Sure enough, there were three black strands of hair between my fingers. I brushed the fur on my jeans and returned to my duty of watching the world go by.

Bozeman swerved to avoid a tumbleweed, and a mile later, we passed the sign welcoming us to Quincey, New Mexico, which was founded in 1861. We passed block after block of one-story houses, then turned left on Main Street.

There was something that always appealed to me about small towns' main drags, but it was something I could never put my finger on. As we headed downtown, the buildings inched closer together, until businesses on entire blocks shared party walls. Had Quincey been a county seat, I'm certain there would've been a courthouse directly in the middle of the town. Since it wasn't, Main Street continued straight through the little burg. We drove past a movie theater that featured *Rear Window* on the marquee. The theater was next to the florist, followed by a clothing store, a hardware store, and a consignment shop. Sometimes I passed the time playing a game in my head where I had to spot certain businesses. Like a diner or a barber, or other establishments that were common to ninety percent of America's tiny towns. Today, though, I simply looked at the buildings as we passed them.

"Where are we supposed to park this beast?" Bozeman asked. It was a valid question since Main Street barely handled the cars already parked along the road. As it was, I was nervous that Bozeman was going to knock off a side mirror or two as we passed cars.

"There's an empty lot behind the bakery. The GPS says the bakery is another two blocks up on the left. Turn left on Jefferson Street, and it will be right on the corner."

Bozeman found Jefferson, turned left, and took a quick left turn into the lot. There was a rusted sign that identified the lot as 'Smith's Motors', but other than the sign, there was no suggestion that a business had ever stood on the property. Bozeman parked the bus and shut it down. He stood and stretched. "Long ride.

I'm glad that's over. When do we meet your friend?"

"We're supposed to meet her for dinner at seven, but since we're so early, I might try to see if I can find her. What are you going to do?"

Bozeman rubbed his chin. "Don't know. I could use some air, so I might take a walk, maybe work on some music."

I nodded, walked to my bedroom, and grabbed my copy of the bus keys, my wallet, and my favorite ball cap. Once I was ready, I said my goodbyes to Gibson and Bozeman and stepped out of the bus. I took a deep breath of New Mexico air, then walked back to Main Street. At the corner, I got a whiff of fresh baked bread from the bakery. My stomach rumbled, and I desired a loaf, but the locked door and the sign told me the store was closed. Dejected, I walked down the sidewalk and did window shopping as I passed a pharmacy, a used bookstore, and a confectioner's shop until I came to the hotel. I noticed a brass plate attached to the building, and I loved learning about history, so I stepped close and read the plaque aloud.

"The Quincey Inn. Established 1862 by John J., Quincey serviced the town along the stagecoach route from Texas to California. The hotel has hosted five presidents, and such notorious figures as Doc Holliday and Butch Cassidy. The Quincey Inn joined New Mexico Register of Historical Places in 1996."

My eyes had barely focused on the last word of the sign when I heard a shrill, excited laugh come from my right side, followed by my name being called.

"Codi Lynn Cassidy!"

I hadn't even turned toward the noise when I saw a flash of long brown hair and I fell into an embrace that knocked the breath from my body.

"Codi! I wasn't expecting to see you until later. I'm so happy you're here."

With some effort, I pulled away from the hug and looked into the beautiful brown eyes of Samantha Henry. "Hi Sam, it's great to see you too. You look great."

I wasn't lying. Sam looked great. Spectacular, actually. She was a good eight inches taller than me. She also had twenty pounds of muscle on me, and had a sparkle in her eyes that never died out, regardless of what she was going through in life.

"What are you doing here so soon?" Sam asked as she hooked her arm into mine and led me away from the hotel and back down the street in the direction I initially came.

"We left earlier than expected, and there wasn't much traffic, so here I am."

"I can't tell you how grateful I am that you came. You know, I never wanted to be on the committee, and I especially didn't want to be in charge of the entertainment. I was thinking of hiring one of the wedding DJs from one of the surrounding cities, but then I thought of you."

Once we got to the corner, Sam fished a set of keys out of her pocket and opened the bakery door. Immediately, the fabulous scent of baked bread enveloped me as she pulled me over the threshold and closed the door behind me. If there was a man-made scent as pleasant as the inside of a bakery, I was yet to find it. As Sam locked the door and set down her keys, I glanced at the display case. My salivary glands kicked into overdrive when I saw the arrangement of pies and muffins in the case. Clearly, I couldn't hide my gaze or my intentions.

"Would you like something?" Sam asked.

"I'd love a muffin. Preferably blueberry."

Sam went around the corner of the counter, took a muffin from the case, and handed it to me. By touch alone, I could tell that it was moist, and it looked like it came right out of a magazine. I took a bite and let out a moan. It was definitely the best muffin I had ever tasted.

"Good?" Sam asked.

I couldn't speak, so I just nodded. I couldn't imagine where she had gotten the blueberries from, but they were the largest, juiciest blueberries I'd ever eaten. She topped the muffin with just a touch of caramelized sugar that added another layer of sweetness and a crunch that added to the overall texture.

"Be right back. You enjoy that." Sam disappeared into the rear of the bakery while I finished the muffin. She appeared three minutes later carrying a sheet pan of pies that she placed on the counter.

"Would you like another muffin?" she asked.

"I'd love another, but I can't. You've seen how once I get started with something like that, I can't stop. The button on my jeans would burst open in an hour."

I dug around in my pocket for some cash. "What do I owe you for the muffin?"

"How about sixty cents?"

Her answer flabbergasted me. "Sixty cents? How do you make a profit selling a muffin for sixty cents?"

Sam smiled. "I won't make a profit on that one. The ingredients run around fifty-three cents, plus labor and whatnot. I usually charge three bucks for a muffin, but consider it the friend discount."

I wanted to argue, but I also didn't want to insult her generosity, so I handed her a dollar. "Thank you. It was wonderful. Keep the change."

Sam accepted the dollar and set it next to the cash register.

"What's with the pies?" I asked.

Sam took a stack of boxes from behind the counter and started boxing up the bakery. "Besides being in charge of entertainment, I'm also on the catering committee."

"Sounds like a lot of work."

Sam shrugged. "It's not too bad. I'm only supplying the bread and the dessert. Rob and Lisa McMurtry from the diner are taking care of the lion's share of the meal."

Sam slipped back around the counter and captured me in a hug again. "It's so good to see you, Codi. I almost didn't recognize you with that hair of yours, but I figured it had to be you."

Ah, yes. My hair. Growing up, I never did like my hair, unlike Sam's, which was a consistent, beautiful brown. Thanks to genetics, I started going gray in my mid-twenties. Since then, I had been dying it practically every color under the rainbow, and at the present time, it was a light blue. You would think that would be off-putting for a country singer. But since I currently had a pixie cut, and I normally wore my cowboy hat when I performed, people rarely noticed, and if they did, no one ever mentioned it.

"How did you find me? I haven't seen you in years."

"Social media. I keep tabs on you. When you broke the top forty and your song was on the radio all the time, I'd tell everyone I talked to you were a friend of mine, but of course, no one believed me." Sam laughed as she stepped back to her pies.

"How did you end up here? I thought you always wanted to be a big-time baker in Manhattan with your own cooking show," I said.

"You, of all people, should know how those dreams work out. I had a place in Atlanta for a few years, but I didn't like it. The bakery was making good money, but most of that was in wedding cakes, and those were something I never enjoyed making. Besides, how many bridezillas can one person deal with before they go nuts? Through some acquaintances I discovered this place was up for sale, so I took a chance, packed my bags, and headed west."

"I'm surprised a town this small would have its own bakery."

"That same thought occurred to me, but I went over the numbers with the previous owner before I took the plunge. I have a contract with the diner to supply their bread and pies. Every morning, I do a pretty good donut and bagel business, and I still make cakes for birthdays and weddings. I'm actually making just as much money as I was in Atlanta, but here, I know all of my customers and can appreciate the small-town life."

I knew what Sam meant about the small-town community.

There was something special about a close-knit group of people that added value to everything. Going to work was much easier when the people you serviced were the people you knew. I even felt that way in my business, even though my small-town community had spread over a dozen states. It wasn't the distance, so much as the people, that, for me, gave it a small-town feel. Every time we put on a show, I recognized a few faces in the crowd.

"So, what are you working on? Can I give you a hand?" I asked.

Sam smiled. "Sure thing. I usually have a woman who works here with me, but she came down with the flu. How good are you at making pies and bread?"

It was my turn to smile. "Well, to be honest, I can bake a cake if I follow directions on the back of the box it came in, and I'm great at putting sliced bread into a toaster. Sometimes I even remember to plug the toaster in before I use it."

Sam motioned for me to follow her into the kitchen. The sight of the stainless-steel appliances, the multiple ovens, and huge bins of flour and sugar immediately overwhelmed me. I swear I saw a wire whisk that was half my height, and a mixing bowl I could probably swim in. I had been inside commercial kitchens before, but this was my first bakery. Once I got done looking around, Sam helped me into an apron and gave me a hairnet.

"You'll want to wear this instead of your cap. You'll never get all the flour off it. How are you with taking things out of the oven, letting them cool down, and then putting them into boxes?" she asked.

Now she was on par with my skill level in the kitchen. "I think I can handle that."

"Great. We've got one more batch to bake up and then we'll head on over to the diner for dinner. You've got a boyfriend, right? He's meeting us for dinner too?"

"He's not my boyfriend, he's my business partner," I said.

It was a common mistake that most people made. Everyone assumed that a man and a woman living on a bus together had to be involved romantically. But for us, it wasn't the case. I admit, Bozeman is a hunk, but he's not my type of hunk, and although we have a musical connection, we never even had a single spark of a romantic one. "I'll call him when we're ready to go over to eat. We're both really interested in hearing what this benefit is all about."

CHAPTER TWO

"What's good here?" Bozeman asked as he set down the menu and looked around to check what other people were eating.

"It's Friday night, so it's the pot roast that usually brings folks in. Meatloaf is pretty good too. Burgers are always a safe bet," Sam said.

"What about the catfish?" I asked.

"I've never had it, but lots of people seem to enjoy that, too."

The server approached the table and dropped off glasses of water for the women and a beer for Bozeman. "Have you decided on what you want for dinner?" she asked with her pen hovering an inch above her order pad.

Sam took a quick drink and set down her glass. "Lisa, this is my friend Codi, and her partner, Bozeman. They're the musicians I booked for tomorrow night. Lisa and her husband, Rob, own this place and are doing the catering for the event."

"Pleased to meet you," Lisa said. She wiped her hand on her apron and shook with Codi and Bozeman. Lisa stood five-seven and had a bright shock of red hair atop her head, and dimples in both cheeks.

"Likewise," I said.

Bozeman tipped his hat in his cowboy way. He preferred to stay in character when out in public.

Bozeman ordered the pot roast, I ordered the meatloaf with a side salad, no dressing, and Sam opted for a burger.

"Codi says we'll be playing during dinner?" Bozeman said after a long draw on his beer.

"For some of it, anyway," Sam said. "The plan is to get the ceremony kicked off. Then, the important folks in the room will be introduced, dinner will start, and we'd like you to play for around twenty minutes. After that, there will be some speeches from the mayor and a couple of others while dessert is served."

"What about after?" Bozeman asked.

"After the dinner, it becomes a little more informal, so you can play for as long as you want to, or rather, as long as the agreed fee lasts. It was four hundred, correct?"

I nodded. "I hate to charge you at all, but we've got to cover our expenses."

"Don't be silly, Codi. Of course you should charge for being here. Everyone who is providing a service is getting paid. It's not a benefit, it's more of an awareness campaign. That reminds me, here." Sam reached around and pulled an envelope from her back pocket. "Here's the cash."

I took the envelope, and without opening it, folded it and shoved it into the front pocket of my jeans. "Thanks. Tell us about the event. What's it about, a fundraiser or something, right?"

"Well, see that guy over there at the table by the window? Wearing jeans and a sport coat and talking like he's trying to draw attention to himself?"

Although Bozeman had a straight view, I had to turn almost all the way around to look at where Sam was pointing with her fork. Near the front window sat a party of five. The man sat in the center of the table, with his back to the window so he could look at everyone in the restaurant. Two people sat on either side of him, and the fellow in question was telling a story more loudly and more animated than the story probably dictated. From where I sat, if I concentrated, I barely heard his voice, but between the distance from him and the other conversations around me, I didn't make out the words. I turned back around to face the people at my table.

"That's Sherman Stier. He's our local real estate mogul. He owns a bunch of land outside of town, and he's trying to get support to build a golf course and resort out there. Those people he's with are potential investors he's brought in from Phoenix, Taos, and Albuquerque. They initially proposed this event to rebuild and rebrand Main Street and generate more tourist business for the town. You know, spiffy things up a little, make this town a stop for people looking to get off the interstate and get a taste of the good old days. The committee has been working on the plan for seven months."

"Who's on the committee?" Bozeman asked.

"Most of the business owners on Main Street, since we're the ones most affected by the increase in tourist traffic. Me, Rob and Lisa, the mayor, the owner of the Quincey Inn, and a few others. You'll meet most of them tomorrow night if you want to. Oh, and Sherman, of course. He's the chair of the committee."

"The mayor isn't the chair?" I asked. "Wouldn't that make the most sense?"

"No, she isn't. Everyone assumed she would be the chairperson, but she declined. She's got enough to worry about trying to run the town. To her credit, she's gotten us pretty far in the three years she's been mayor. Did you notice the potholes on Main Street when you drove in?"

Bozeman leaned forward in his chair. "I don't recall seeing any."

"That's because after probably a good twenty years of complaining, the new mayor got them all patched up. Even installed pretty cobblestone crosswalks at every intersection around downtown. She's also been working hard at getting the local schools updated, and the water quality improved."

"She sounds like a go-getter," I said.

Sam nodded. "Sure is. She would've been the perfect choice to lead the committee. Unfortunately, we're stuck with Sherman."

"Is he doing a terrible job?" I asked.

"Let's say he has a tendency to push things in directions that will benefit him the most."

"Like the golf course?" I asked.

Sam nodded. "Exactly like that. Although he claims that bringing people into his resort will be good for the town too. A rising tide and all that."

I spied Lisa approaching with a tray of food. Behind her trailed a tall, thin man in a chef's coat. While Lisa passed out our food, she introduced her husband. "Rob, this here is Codi and Bozeman. They're the singers for tomorrow."

Rob offered his hand. "Glad to meet you," he said. As Lisa finished food distribution, Rob simply stared at me. After a moment, he scratched his buzz-cut head and walked away.

Lisa's cheeks turned red from embarrassment. "You'll have to excuse him. He's a little shy around celebrities."

I spotted him rushing back from the kitchen with his phone in hand. "I'm not really a celebrity. And he can't be that shy. He's coming back."

Rob reached the table and turned his phone so I recognized the person on the screen. "Is this you?"

It only took me a glance to determine he had pulled up the video of my one hit song. It was an excellent song, but I always hated the video. The producer headed in a much different creative direction than I wanted to, but I was only a kid and didn't have a clue what was going on, so what did I know? "Yep, that's me."

Rob smiled widely. "I knew that was you the second I saw you. My gosh. I loved that video. Can I get a selfie with you? And maybe an autograph?"

In my peripheral vision, I saw Bozeman smirk. He wasn't

big on being approached by fans, but I didn't mind. I always figured it was the fans who bought CDs and tickets and other merchandise. It was the fans who showed up at county fairs and other gigs. It was the fans who waited for the show in heat or cold or rain. I never turned a fan away. "Of course."

I stood and pushed away from the table, and I stepped closer to Rob and put my arm around him. Rob handed the phone to Lisa. Since there was a good foot's height difference between Rob and me, Lisa had to back up almost into the lap of the person at the table behind her. After a few photos, Lisa shooed Rob back to the kitchen.

"I'm so sorry about that," Lisa said.

"No worries, it happens all the time. I've got some promo photos on the bus. I'll sign one of those for him and give it to him at the event tomorrow," I said.

"That would make his day," Lisa said. "I'll leave you to dinner. If y'all need anything, just call."

I retook my seat and adjusted myself in front of the meatloaf and dug in. I was famished, despite the giant muffin I had eaten earlier.

"That happen often?" Sam asked. "Getting asked for pictures and autographs?"

"It all depends. Usually on show nights I'll get asked for a dozen or more, and occasionally someone will recognize me out in public and ask, but most people will leave me alone. I don't really mind, though. It's all a part of the business. The way you bake those muffins, people should ask for your autograph."

Sam laughed, put down her burger, and wiped her fingers on the napkin. "Well, I get asked for recipes now and then, but that's not quite the same thing."

"Sure, it is," I said. "You provide something that people love, and they want to share that experience. Do you ever give them the recipes?"

Sam leaned in until our foreheads almost touched. "Yes, but to be honest, it's not the complete recipe. I always leave out the secret ingredients, so their version never comes out quite like mine. Nothing to make the recipe fail, mind you, just something that will make their finished product just a little different from mine."

"That's really smart," I said. "Keeps them coming back for yours."

"My thoughts exactly."

Bozeman finished his meal, drained his beer, and stood. "Excuse me, ladies. I have some work to finish on the bus. It was nice to meet you, Sam. I look forward to seeing you again tomorrow." Bozeman winked at her, then walked toward the door.

"He likes you," I said.

"How can you tell?" Sam asked.

"We've been partners for a long time. I could tell just by how he wouldn't stop jabbering."

Sam took the last bite of her burger and washed it down. "Jabbering? I don't think he said over six sentences."

"Yeah, but that's a lot for him. He's the strong, silent type. You'll see more of his personality on the stage tomorrow night."

"Didn't he just leave you with the bill? Shouldn't the cowboy pay? Is chivalry dead?" Sam asked.

"Not in this case. Whether he pays, or I do, it comes from the same business account. So, consider it a company expense," I said.

"Ah, gotcha. That makes sense. You didn't eat your salad."

"Oh, yeah, thanks for the reminder." I pulled a plastic gallon-sized bag from my pocket, and discretely as possible, dumped the salad into the bag and sealed it up.

Sam looked at me like I had a third arm sprouting from my chin.

"It's for my pets," I explained as I set the salad next to the leg of my chair.

Sam looked like she didn't believe me.

I was about to offer a more in-depth explanation about the

kids when someone slipped into Bozeman's chair.

"Hi," the man said. He was wearing a Toronto Blue Jays windbreaker and hat to match.

"Codi Cassidy, meet Dean Williams," Sam said. "Dean is our local historian."

"In training," Dean said as he shook my hand. "Fourth generation, actually. My great-grandfather started it, and it just got passed down from there."

"I would've figured you for a tourist," I said.

"Nah, I'm just a big baseball fan. Just got home last week from my yearly pilgrimage to baseball parks. This year I hit Toronto, Detroit, Cleveland, and Cincinnati. I'm trying to get to a game at every stadium. I'm about halfway there."

"That's interesting," I said.

"Are you in town for the big event?" Dean asked.

"She's the singer," Sam said.

"No kidding. I look forward to the show then. Hey, listen, can I take Sam away for a minute or two? Just some committee members' stuff."

I opened my mouth to reply, but Sam beat me to it. "That's rude. Whatever you can say to me, you can say in front of her. She's my friend."

Dean looked at me. "I meant no offense." He turned back to Sam. "It's not about her overhearing. It's just kind of busy in here, don't you think?"

I saw the almost imperceptible shift of his head toward the front table. Sam caught it too.

"Oh. I understand. Yes, it is loud in here. Let's go outside and talk for a moment. Codi, I'll be right back, okay?"

I smiled my best smile. "Of course. Take your time."

Dean took Sam by the hand and led the way, and I turned my head to watch them leave the diner. Then I shifted into Bozeman's seat, so I had a better view of the place. Like Bozeman, I always preferred a seat with my back to the wall so I could monitor everything going on around me. It wasn't a cowboy thing, but something my father had taught me.

Brian Cassidy, my father, was a detective for as long as I could remember. He worked for the Denver Police Department, and since I was an inquisitive kid, I always had questions about the cases he worked on. Although he would divulge no personal information, so I never knew the 'who', he always shared the tips and tricks he used to figure out who the criminal was. During that time, I also had a love of police procedurals on television. We would watch those together and he would tell me what would work in real life, and what would work only in Hollywood. By the time I got to my teens, we'd discuss his cases, and I would tell him what I would do if I were the detective. More often than not, I was on the right track of what clues to look for. By far, the biggest skill he taught me was the power of observation. He often said that I could learn more at a crime scene, just sitting in a chair and watching a suspect pool than I could with all the fancy DNA evidence shown on TV. He said that's where most shows got it wrong. The detective's job was narrowing the suspect list until it was down to just one, and it was the court's job to prove it.

My mom, Christina Cassidy, was where I got my love of music from. It was mom who taught me the guitar and the piano. She was the one who got me into music theory and songwriting, and it was she who first supported my first public appearance at my ninth-grade talent show. In the summer when school was out, mom would let me travel with her to local shows. I'd help set up her equipment, or change her guitar strings, or run lines for the amps. I learned from her all about stage presence and how to work with an audience, and how to create a set list to keep the crowd from being bored. Interestingly enough, she also taught me about the power of observation. She drilled into my head that when on stage, I always had to be aware of who was out there and what they were doing. You never knew if someone was going to cause trouble. And when trouble started, it was best to grab the guitar and head backstage if the venue had one, or head for the door if it didn't.

I didn't really know what she meant, but the more shows I went to, the more shows I spent sitting in the wings and watching the audience while listening to her. I could tell who was there to have fun, who had a little too much to drink, who was looking for love, and who was looking for trouble.

I learned a lot of lessons from both my parents, lessons that I still carried with me and worked to hone every time I was out in public or up on a stage.

What I learned while I was sitting alone at the diner waiting for Sam to return was that people didn't seem to care for Mr. Sherman Stier. As the locals entered or left the diner, they stopped at other tables to share handshakes with friends. I noticed several friendly slaps on the back, and a bunch of quick snippets of conversations, but none with Sherman. In fact, most people seemed to avoid his table altogether. That didn't seem quite right to me, and I wondered why, but since I had no one to ask, I held onto my question in my head.

I saw Lisa approaching the table, so I emptied my glass of water and put on a smile.

"I'm sorry to bother you, Ms. Codi. Sam called and said she'd be away for longer than expected, so she asked me to tell you not to wait for her."

"Okay. Thank you. If give me the bill, I'll settle up and be on my way then."

Lisa waved her hands back and forth as if trying to ward off a demon. "No. There's no charge. If Rob heard I made his favorite country star pay for dinner, I'd never hear the end of it. He'd bug me about it from now until judgment day."

I reached into my pocket for my wallet. "At least let me leave you a tip, then. The service was excellent."

Lisa begged that off as well. "No. Please. If you can remember that signed photo for Rob, and that will more than make up for a tip."

I put my wallet back. "Thank you so much, but please, the next time I'm here, I'll pay like any other customer."

Lisa nodded and left to check on the other tables. I grabbed my bagged salad and left the diner.

The diner was only two blocks from the bakery, so we had walked there. It was a beautiful New Mexico night. The stars were coming out, and the moon was bright. I would've loved to get out into the desert and away from the city lights to really appreciate the night sky, but I knew I had other things to do. As I walked to the bakery, I passed the historical museum, which was on the opposite side of the street. I noticed downstairs all the lights were out, but on the second floor, there was a light on. Although someone had drawn the curtains, I could see animated shadows pacing back and forth in front of the window, as if in a heated discussion. I couldn't help but wonder if that was Sam and Dean. Were they lovers having a quarrel? Was there something else going on? Either way, it wasn't my business.

It was just after seven the next morning, and I was sitting outside the bus on my favorite lawn chair with Merle on my lap. He was a playful fellow who enjoyed getting his belly scratched. From where I was sitting, I saw Sam come out of the bakery's back door and walk toward me with her head down. It was body language I remembered from long ago when we hung out together. Sam was feeling penitent. She stopped a couple feet in front of me, lifted her chin, and looked me in the eye.

"I'm sorry about leaving you alone in the diner last night. Dean and I had some … committee business to discuss."

I thought about letting her go on, and giving her the business about her ditching me, but honestly, I couldn't do it. I was never one to hold grudges, especially over something so minor. "It's okay. I understand."

Sam took a step closer. "That's a pretty cat."

At that moment, Merle did a circle in my lap, revealing his striped tail before settling back down.

Sam took two steps backward. "Is that a skunk?"

I lifted him up so she could see him better. "This is Merle. Don't worry, he can't spray. Come, say hello."

Sam didn't move.

"Come on, you chicken, he's okay. Come feed him a tomato and he'll be your friend forever." I reached for the salad bag at my feet, extracted a couple of cherry tomatoes, and held them for Sam to take.

Merle watched the transaction with great interest as Sam took the fruit from my hands and took a hesitant step closer. She held out a tomato, and Merle reached forward with his paws, grabbed it from her, and nibbled at it. A drop of tomato juice appeared on his chin, and I wiped it away without thinking about it.

"Why in the world do you have a pet skunk?" Sam asked.

"I rescued him from a vet when I had to take my cat in for a tooth removal. He was in the cage right next to Gibson, and they looked almost like twins, so I took them both home. Skunks are smart and sociable animals. You can scratch his belly if you like."

"Thanks, I'll pass on that. You have a cat and a skunk? Do they get along okay?" Sam gave Merle the second tomato, who had made quick work of the first one.

I nodded. "You should see them together. I think they think the other is part of their own species. For most of the time, they all get along fine."

"All?"

"See anything interesting under the front fender of the bus?"

Sam bent at the waist, looked for several seconds, and straightened. "Is that a raccoon?"

I nodded. "That's Dolly, the famous three-legged raccoon. She's part of the family, but you'll want to watch your wallet around her. Despite being down a paw, she's a formidable pickpocket. Willie and Waylon are somewhere around here, too. They're a couple of chipmunks who live in a nest in a rusted-out spot in the back of my bus."

"And you travel with this menagerie?"

"Yep, we're one big, happy family." I lifted Merle from my

lap and set him on the ground. He nuzzled my leg with his nose, then went off to join Dolly under the bus. "What's the plan today?"

"I've got bread and a couple pies to bake for tonight, and then I have to be at the event early to set up."

"What time can I get into the venue? We have to set up and do a sound check."

"I'll be there around four, so you can come anytime you want after that. It's being held in the hall of the First Baptist Church, which is about five blocks from here. Go down to Adams, turn right, and you can't miss it from there. It's the only enormous church on that street. There's a small lot in the back, and I'll cone off some room for your bus so people don't park there."

"I appreciate that. You need any help?" I asked.

"You have nothing you need to do for your show?"

"Not really. We worked out the set list last night, and I'd like to go over it with you to see if there're any changes you'd like. Other than that, all I need to do is restring a guitar, but that won't take any more time than fifteen minutes," I said.

"Well, come along then. We'll talk about the music, and I'll make a baker out of you."

Somehow, I doubted that.

CHAPTER THREE

I got up from my chair, dumped the remains of the salad into the bowl Merle and Dolly were eating from, and followed Sam into the bakery. When I walked in the door, I expected to have to set things up from scratch to begin the day. To my surprise, there were already dozens of dinner rolls cooling on racks, and more rising.

"In about ten minutes, those pies can come out of the oven," Sam said as she donned an apron. "After you're finished with that, there's a blueberry muffin up front that needs eating, so I'd appreciate it if you would do something about that as well. Since you're helping me out, you can keep the dollar."

I didn't bother to hide my smile. "If you insist. What time did you get here?"

"About four. I open the doors at eight, so I always get here early to make the donuts and bagels. Once the morning rush is gone, I make the dinner breads and desserts for the diner, and slide in any special orders I have."

"You sound like you're always busy."

"A baker's life is never idle." Sam basted some melted

butter over a sheet of unbaked rolls and slid them into the oven. "Probably just like yours, right?"

I thought about it. We spent the vast majority of our time on the road, just getting from one place to another. Bozeman and I both wrote songs and practiced playing music, both separately and together. But because of the simple nature of our business, we did those things anytime we wanted. The only real committed time we had to be anywhere was any time we contracted for. That time would range anywhere from one to four hours, including the time spent on sound checks and selling merchandise afterward. "No, I got the better end of the deal. I couldn't even imagine working as hard as you do."

Sam put her hands on her hips. "It's not that bad. I take every Sunday off, and Saturdays too in the winter. And all the major holidays, of course. Although, I do put in extra hours before Thanksgiving, Christmas, and Valentine's Day. As you can probably guess, I always have lots of orders for those. I don't mind, though. I wouldn't give up being a baker for anything, not even for being a famous country star like you. By the way, you've got flour on your nose, superstar."

I thought she was kidding, so I grabbed a stainless steel mixing bowl and checked out my reflection. Son of a gun. "How did that get there? I didn't touch a thing yet."

Sam chuckled. "It's a workplace hazard. Trust me, that flour dust can get into places you wouldn't want me to mention."

I was about to tell her I needed no further information when the back door opened and a woman entered. Physically, she looked to be in her late thirties or early forties, but the weariness on her face made her appear older. Aftereffects of a severe illness, I thought. Like Sam, she dressed in jeans and a T-shirt with the bakery's name emblazoned on it.

"Hey, Shanna. This is my friend, Codi Cassidy. Feeling better?"

"Hi Codi. Nice to meet you. Yes. Sorry I wasn't able to be here for the last few days. It was a struggle to even get out of bed.

I wasn't even sure if I would be in today."

"I told you before, if you're sick, stay away. We certainly don't want you sneezing all over the pastries you're serving to customers. Shanna runs the front of the house for me, and I'm teaching her some of my tricks of the trade as well."

Shanna donned a fresh apron and disappeared to the front. I overheard some shuffling, and the cash register opening and closing. Shanna moved back and forth, grabbing bakery items for the display cases. The timer dinged, so I pulled four pies out of the oven and placed them gently on the cooling racks. All four were Dutch Apple, my second favorite pie, after only a fluffy Boston Creme.

"Better get that muffin before Shanna sells it," Sam said.

Taking Sam's advice, I rushed to the front, where I found the muffin sitting on a napkin next to the register.

"I sensed you coming," Shanna explained.

The bakery had three small wrought-iron tables common in old ice cream parlors, and each table sat two, so I took my muffin to one and sat down.

"Want something to drink with that?" Shanna asked.

"Water would be fine." I half expected to get a simple cup of water, but Shanna presented me with a chilled bottle. I opened the bottle, then took a swig. Chilled was fine, but I actually preferred my water at room temperature, but I wouldn't tell her that. "Thanks. Do you enjoy working here?" I removed the liner from the muffin, broke off a piece of the bottom, and ate it. It was just as delicious as I remembered from the day before.

"It's a great place, and I can't imagine working anywhere else. I got lucky. I just got back to town a couple of months ago after being away for a few years. You see, I had to escape from a… toxic relationship, so when I came home, I had to find work. Sam found out about my hard-luck story and asked me to work here. I really like it. I'm thinking of opening my very own bakery someday. Sam's been a godsend, and I don't know what I would've done without her." Shanna disappeared for a few minutes, then returned with a tray of donuts that she placed in the case.

While I worked on my muffin, I looked outside and saw Sherman Stier across the street with the four fellows he entertained for dinner the night before. Directly across from the bakery was a small artist's gallery. I saw it was closed since there was a big red 'closed' sign in the front window that I noticed from my seat. It seemed the group of men were more interested in the actual building than the shop inside. One turned down the corner and studied the building, as if he was accounting for each brick in the structure. At one point, he reached up, touched the stone, then looked at his fingers. After a few minutes, they regrouped, and Sherman pointed in my direction. Without stopping to look for traffic, the men marched across the street. I checked the clock on the wall over Shanna's shoulder. The bakery didn't open for another twenty minutes.

Sherman peered in the window, saw us inside, and rapped on the door. A bit of anger flashed through Shanna's hazel eyes, and she sighed heavily. She took a moment to compose herself before she opened the door a crack and slipped into her best professional voice. "I'm sorry, we don't open until eight."

Sherman pushed his way through the door, and aggressively stomped into the bakery like a lowland gorilla showing its dominance. "I'm not here for food. I'd like to talk to the owner."

Shanna took an involuntary step backward. "You know what her name is."

I tried to stay invisible and eat my muffin while Shanna fetched Sam from the back.

Sam came from the back, wiping her hands on a towel as she approached. "Can I help you?"

Sherman stepped forward with no introductions for his colleagues. "I'll come right down to it. We'd like to buy this building. As you've heard, there's a resort and golf community going up outside of town. We'd like to make sure we have a presence within town itself, and what better place to have it than right here on Main Street?"

"We've talked about this before, with the same answer. The bakery is not for sale." Sam said.

Sherman took another half-step closer to her. Apparently, he wasn't used to being turned down. "I'm not interested in the bakery, just the building. Everything is for sale. Just tell me your asking price, and we can get this deal done."

"And what am I supposed to do with the bakery? This is my livelihood."

"Surely you can move it to another part of town."

"No way. There's been a bakery at this location since they founded this town. I'm not moving."

"Well, I'm sure we would find you a position at the new resort. In management perhaps? Better hours, better pay, benefits, vacation time."

"No deal. Please leave. I have customers to serve soon."

Sherman leaned in close to Sam and whispered soft enough I had to strain to pick it up. "I will get this building. You and your precious bakery can't stop the wheels of progress." Sherman turned, left the building, and escorted his party down the street to the next target on his wish list.

Sam closed the door and locked it behind him.

"Nice guy," I said.

Sam shook her head. "He's a prince. He rolled into town about three years ago and started buying up properties like mad. At first, it wasn't a big deal because he seemed to go for tracts of lands that had for sale signs on them forever. He bought defunct farms and businesses and other properties like that outside of the city limits that no one else wanted. Within the last few months, he started focusing on properties in town. Clearly there's a plan there, but I can't guess what it is. All I understand is people aren't happy."

"Why?" I asked.

"Partially because he's an outsider. You get how small

towns can be, right? Hard to fit in? I've been here for eight years, and it's only been within the last year or two that people have warmed up to me."

I wiped away the crumbs from my shirt. "The muffins probably help."

Sam laughed. "You're probably right. Yes, I'm an outsider, but I provide a service that the people want, so I'm sure that has helped. Stier, on the other hand, just pushed his way in, without trying to fit in, which hasn't endeared him to many people. The townsfolk here like what they've built, and are resistant to any big changes."

A timer dinged in the back, so Sam excused herself. I took a moment to make sure I hadn't left a mess, and Shanna returned to stocking donuts.

Shanna took one last look to make sure everything was ready to open. Satisfied, she unlocked the door and turned on the neon sign that declared the bakery was ready for business, then stepped behind the display case. "I sure hope she doesn't sell this place. That would be bad for everyone. Especially me."

The door opened and an elderly woman entered, followed by a mom with two toddlers in tow.

"I'll get out of your way," I said. I stopped in the back and said goodbye to Sam, and headed out the back door and returned to my favorite lawn chair next to the bus. Curious about what they were up to, I looked for Merle and Dolly, but neither was in sight. Since skunks and raccoons are both nocturnal, I assumed they had settled in for a long day's nap. They normally spent the daytime in the special converted storage compartment beneath the bus they called home. I picked up a skitter, then saw two brown flashes of fur, so I assumed Willie and Waylon were out enjoying the day.

Bozeman's boots clunked down the bus steps, and he set up his chair next to mine.

"Have you been off with your friend?" Bozeman asked before he sipped a steaming mug of coffee.

"Yep. She's turning me into a baker."

Bozeman laughed. "That ain't gonna happen."

I grinned. He was right. I worked a six-string just fine but put me in front of a recipe card and I was hopeless.

"Does she have a husband or boyfriend you know of?"

I thought about that for a second. She hadn't said, and I hadn't asked, although I should have, if only to be polite.

"You'll have to find that out for yourself. You can ask her tonight. I wouldn't bother her now."

"What's going on, Codi? You got that look on your face, along with flour on your nose."

I wiped my face. "Which look is that?" I asked, although I already had the answer. This was a conversation we've had on more than one occasion, but since it was like a comedy routine we followed, I played my part.

"It looks like you're going to go out looking for trouble," Bozeman said.

"You know me. I don't have to go looking for trouble. It's there in the morning waiting for me when I wake up."

"You got one of your special feelings?"

"Yeah. There's something not quite right going on here, and I think Sam is right in the middle of it. She didn't outright say anything, but she's not the type to spill all her problems on anyone over a beer."

"Or it might be nothing."

"I considered that too. It could be the stress of the party tonight combined with working too hard. Honestly, I don't comprehend how she does it all."

"It's got to be tough on her, especially if she doesn't have a man."

I leaned over and slapped Bozeman's leg. "Slow down there, cowboy. I never said she didn't have a man. And although we like to wear our tall hats and dusty boots, this isn't the nineteenth century. Women are perfectly capable of living life without a man around."

Bozeman chuckled. "Yeah, I'd like to see you live your life without me."

I sent a sarcastic chuckle right back at him. "That's only because you drive the bus and carry all the heavy stuff, but even then, I could find someone else to that in half a heartbeat."

Bozeman was silent for a minute. "No, you couldn't."

I capitulated. "Yeah, you're probably right. Hey, do me a favor, will you? Keep an eye out for any funny business tonight, okay?"

"I always do." Bozeman pushed out of his chair and stretched. "I'm a might hungry. I think I'm going to head over yonder for something to eat."

As I smiled, I shook my head. Once Bozeman caught a scent, he was on it like a hound dog. Usually he caught his prey, since he was a good-looking man with his rugged looks, six-pack abs, and scruffy beard. I didn't know why women ever fell for his cowboy act, but he played the part well, and bless his heart for it.

"Bring me back a muffin if they have any," I yelled to him. Bozeman lifted a hand to acknowledge me, then slipped around the corner of the building.

I got out of my chair, checked on Merle and Dolly, and stepped onto the bus. I walked to the equipment storage room and pulled out my favorite guitar. After I rummaged around in a drawer for a fresh set of strings, I started into the pep talk I had with myself before every show. "Don't worry, everything will be fine. You and your guitar will be in tune, you'll get no amp feedback, and you won't forget any chords or lyrics. The show will flow as smooth as room temperature butter over a slice of fresh toast. Not a single thing will go wrong."

I used the same mantra before every show, and every single time I thought about changing that last line. It seemed often, things not only went wrong, but flew completely off the tracks.

A little after four in the afternoon, I made sure all the pets were aboard and Bozeman drove the bus the short distance to the church. I would've preferred to walk, but we would have had to make several trips lugging all our gear. As promised, there was an area in the church lot marked off by traffic cones, and I stacked them up while Bozeman parked the bus. As Bozeman started gathering the equipment we needed, I approached the church to determine where we were supposed to go.

A cinder block was leaning against the church's back door, holding it open. I considered that an invitation, so I passed through the entry and followed the hallway past several dark classrooms. At the end of the corridor, I had a choice of left or right, and I trusted my intuition, turned right, and within a few yards, came to the empty sanctuary. Since my intuition failed me, I backtracked and eventually entered the large space that doubled as a gymnasium and meeting space. The far end of the area contained a small, raised stage, and atop the stage was an upright piano and a drum set. I hoped no one planned to sit in with us.

"Can I help you?"

I turned around and found myself almost eye to eye with the man before me. He was short in stature, only two inches taller than me, and he wore dark jeans and a light green polo shirt.

I smiled and stuck out my hand. "Hello. I'm Codi Cassidy. I'm the singer for tonight."

The man eyed me for a few seconds without speaking a word. I'm pretty sure it was the blue hair that distracted him.

"I'm Pastor Tom Percy and I'm sorry if I startled you."

"You didn't. Sam told me she'd be here after four to set up."

"I'm here, I'm here," Sam said as she entered the room, lugging two large plastic bins filled with dinner rolls. "Sorry I'm a little late. Anyone else here yet?"

Pastor Tom took one bin from her and carried it to a table. "No. Just us and the singer."

There was something icy about his tone, but I didn't know why, and at the time I didn't care. "I can come back a little later," I said.

"No, you're good," Sam said.

"Am I on the stage tonight?" I asked, not wanting to assume anything.

"Yes. We can push the piano back a bit if it's in your way. We'll need to save a little room up front for the dignitary speeches," Sam said.

"Y'all can use my mic for that if you need to. I'll go grab my gear."

I excused myself and left the room. Because my sense of direction is just as bad as my intuition, I backtracked to the wrong hallway. I could tell I headed toward the church's main entrance instead of the back door based on the signs I passed. I figured I'd simply exit the building and walk around the outside instead of venturing through the labyrinth again. As I got closer, I heard two people arguing.

"I'm telling you; something has to be done about him." The man's voice echoed through the deserted hall. It sounded familiar, but I couldn't put a face to the voice.

"I agree with you. Keep your voice down. This is a church, and someone will hear you," came the reply. It was a woman speaking, one I hadn't met before.

The statements dropped to a whisper, so I could no longer hear the words, but I could tell by the cadence and the tone that it wasn't a pleasant conversation. I took another step, rounded a corner, and found the couple arguing just inside the front door. The woman stopped in mid-sentence when I approached, and they both looked at me. Both of their countenances switched from furrowed brows and frowns to bright eyes and smiles in an instant. I'd seen that reaction lots of times. They came from people who internally buried their current thoughts and moods, especially around strangers. They put on a smiling face in order to hide the conflict.

"Cassie, right?" the man said as he stepped forward and offered his hand. "Good to see you again."

"Codi," I said. I couldn't place him.

He could read the non-recognition in my face. "Dean

Williams? Local historian? I met you at the diner last night?"

It clicked. He was the one who rushed Sam away from me.

"Dean. Blue Jays fan. Of course. And you are?"

A silver-haired woman stepped forward. "Reba Chestnut."

"Reba owns the bed-and-breakfast over on Third Street. It's a lovely place. You should stay when you get a chance."

"We're all booked up through Labor Day," Reba interjected. "Summer's our busy time."

Dean moved a step closer to Reba and held his fist to his mouth. "Not for long."

Reba threw him an icicle stare, then turned and rushed from the church.

Dean gave me an awkward chuckle. "You'll have to forgive her. She's stressed about the event tonight, although I don't know why. She's only in charge of the decorations. In her state, she can't take on much more. Where are you headed?"

"Um. I was going to the back parking lot, but I got turned around."

"Happens all the time if you're not used to this building. They didn't do the best job with the layout when they added on from the original church. Follow me, I'll take you."

Without waiting for a reply, Dean marched forward, and I got into step behind him. We passed the gymnasium, and within two minutes he was holding open the back door for me even though he didn't need to since the cinder block was still in place. Outside the bus, I saw a small pile of gear, and Bozeman was carrying an amplifier down the bus steps.

"How does it look?" he asked once I got within speaking range.

"Pretty typical. Small stage. Room is a converted gym, so we should be able to get by without the full sound system."

Bozeman nodded, then stepped back into the bus for more gear. While he was gone, I opened the storage compartment nearest the door and wrestled our portable luggage cart to the ground. I flipped up the handle and transferred the gear on the ground to it. The little cart wouldn't haul everything we'd need at once, but it would save effort and energy from lugging everything by hand.

Bozeman reappeared, toting one of his guitars. "Here, take this and I'll pull the cart."

We switched tasks, and I led Bozeman to the door, down the hall, and into the gym. He stopped just inside the door and looked around, saying nothing. From experience, I could tell he was mentally mapping out the space. I knew he was thinking of where the best speaker placement would be to get the best sound throughout the room. He also considered if we should bother setting up our lighting rig, and a million other trivial details. He even went to the level of determining the floor composition and what material they made the walls of. The man knew his acoustics.

Bozeman glanced at me, pulled the cart to the stage, and together we unloaded the gear. Bozeman's eyes looked over the gear for a moment, then he nodded and took the cart out for another load. While he was gone, I took an assessment of my own and decided the piano would indeed need to move. I jumped onto the stage and gave the piano a nudge, but it didn't move an inch. I looked at the casters, saw that they were unlocked, and I tried again. It wouldn't budge. It was clearly the heaviest piano ever made.

CHAPTER FOUR

"The locks are backward."

I turned around and spotted a short, plump man standing before me. He wore blue jeans, a checkered shirt that reminded me of a tablecloth, and a light brown sports coat with a carnation pinned to the lapel.

"Hanson Johns. I own the flower shop up the block." He thrust a meaty hand forward, and I shook it.

"Codi Cassidy. What did you say about the locks?"

"Someone installed them backward. Unlocked means locked, and the reverse."

I looked down and stepped on one lock, then the other. I already detected a noticeable difference in the way the large instrument handled.

"Let me help with that." Hanson stepped over and took a side. Together, we rolled it to the back wall and reset the locks. "You need a pianist tonight? I'm quite good." Without waiting for an answer, Hanson sat behind the piano and played a little Mozart for me. He was right, he played well.

"That was fantastic. Do you know any country songs?" I

asked.

Hanson said nothing, but his reddening ears told me all I needed to know.

I smiled. "Tell you what, you learn some country tunes, and the next time we come through you can sit in with us, okay?"

I overheard someone clear his throat. I turned around and caught a look from Pastor Tom that told me he didn't seem happy. "Hanson, come on. We need your help."

Hanson blushed again and left the stage in a hurry.

Bozeman returned with a second load, dropped the gear off, and left again. Included in the pile sat my laptop, that played an essential role in our operation. I opened the laptop and placed it on top of the piano. The laptop contained all the programming for our show, and, other than my music, was the thing I had the most pride in. I had cobbled together a program that would run a lighting and sound system for any set list I selected. Besides lights and sound balances, it also provided the remaining members of the band.

We had backing tracks included in there for much of the music we performed. I had everything from fiddles, to slide guitars, to banjos, to our electronic drummer that I had affectionately named Ringo. Usually, some in the music circle frowned on the backing tracks, but I liked them because they gave the act a much richer sound than only the two of us provided. And I made it a point to mention that what the audience viewed on stage was the real deal. I sang, and Bozeman did background vocals, and we each played our instruments in real time. Usually, the first couple of numbers we did were acoustic ones, so the audience understood it was us doing the work. Once I brought in the backing tracks later, they didn't distract from the performance. I had set up most of the gig beforehand, but I had a few variables to plug into the program. I needed to turn off the lighting options and enter the rough dimensions of the room. The rest I'd adjust during the sound check.

When I turned around, I spotted Bozeman who had returned and seemed busy setting up the PA system we used on smaller gigs. He attached a cable and tossed the other end to me, which I caught on the fly and plugged into the laptop. Bozeman positioned the speakers while I followed him and ran the cables and electrical. After that, he got out his guitar and fussed with all his pedals. I set out the guitar and microphone stands, then the microphones, then hooked up the remaining cables to tie it all together.

Bozeman sat, tuning his guitar, and I checked the space for mine. "Where's my Martin?"

Bozeman looked up. "You tell me. I didn't see it in the locker, so I have no clue."

I slapped my hand against my forehead. "That's right. It's on my bed. I'll come right back. Are we missing anything else?"

Bozeman glanced around the area, shook his head no, then returned to his tuning.

I jumped from the stage and rushed out to the bus. My Martin laid right where I had put it when I restrung it. I slipped it into its case and closed it up. As I stepped from the bus, I noticed a delivery van parked three spots over. The back door stood open, and I saw Hanson removing a large box, which I assumed contained flowers or table centerpieces. Next to Hanson stood Rob, and I noticed Rob wasn't happy about something because he kept jabbing Hanson in the shoulder. From my position, I noticed the back of Hanson's neck redden. Hanson handed Rob the box, then removed one for himself. He used his hip to close the van door, and they both disappeared into the church.

I set my guitar case on the ground and reentered the bus. From a small file cabinet in the gear room, I took out a glossy promotional photo, scribbled a message and my signature on it, and left the bus.

When I returned to the gymnasium, I placed the photo on the piano next to the computer and opened my guitar case and checked the tuning. Once my guitar and the rest of the gear sounded up to my standards, I looked over at Bozeman.

"Ready for a sound check?" I asked.

In typical Bozeman fashion, he nodded and powered on all the equipment and made sure everything worked properly. He gave me the thumbs up, and I approached my microphone. "Hey everyone. We're going to do a quick sound check."

I did a four-count and together we launched into a Lee Ann Womack song. As I sang, I looked out at the audience, which comprised those setting up the room for the event. I saw Sam and Dean straightening tables and laying down tablecloths. Hanson placed floral arrangements on each table. Lisa and Rob arranged place settings, and Pastor Tom helped Reba put up red, white, and blue bunting on the walls to add a little more color to the spartan gym. There were other people I didn't know doing various chores, but I saw everything was coming together bit by bit.

Once Bozeman felt his gear was working fine, he stepped off the stage and stood in various areas of the room and watched me play. He came back, made minor adjustments to the speakers, and changed the volume on the PA, then returned to the far wall. He listened intently as I repeated a chorus and gave me the thumbs up. I stopped playing, turned on the computer, and started a backing track. Bozeman stayed at his location, then soon gave me a second thumbs up. I turned off the track and stepped back to the microphone.

"Thanks everyone. That'll do it for now."

It did not surprise me when I got a smattering of applause and a random 'woo-hoo' from someone I didn't recognize. I set my guitar on the stand and turned off the electronics until show time.

"Did everything sound okay?" I asked Bozeman when he returned to the stage.

"As good as it can. It's not the Ryman, but it'll do for this show."

I was about to respond when I sensed a loud crash. I looked up just in time to spot Sam racing out of the gym with Dean hot on her heels. The amazing thing was everyone else in the room went back to what they were doing, as if Sam's actions were a normal occurrence.

"I'll be right back," I said to Bozeman, then rushed out of the room without trying to look like I was rushing out of the room.

With haste, I exited the church and looked around the parking lot, but I spotted neither Sam nor Dean. I caught a commotion from the sidewalk, and even before I reached the end of the building, I heard voices.

"Sam, I'm telling you, we all agree. We have to do something about him before it's too late. We have to act. Now. As soon as possible," Dean said.

"And I'm telling you, I can't go along with you. That's not me."

"It's not me, either. Or Lisa, or Hanson, or any of the others. But there's no other choice. Do you really want to lose your bakery? That means everything to you."

There came a long pause, a perfect chance to step around the corner and announce my presence, but something held me back. I didn't want it to seem like I was eavesdropping, but on the other hand, I had an instinct to jump in feet first to protect my friend. I waited.

Sam's voice seemed quieter, yet more intense. "I won't lose my bakery. Ever. We'd better get back in there. We somehow need to make it through this sideshow of an evening. Then we can figure out what to do."

I took that as my cue. I felt like a kid listening in on my parents, and I didn't want to get caught, so I ran as fast as I could to the bus, threw open the door, and scrambled up the steps. As I caught my breath, I looked out a window and spotted Sam and Dean walking around the corner. Dean went on ahead while Sam stood and stared in my direction, and I wondered if they had caught me.

From the kitchen, I loaded a cooler with a half dozen bottles of water, caught my breath, and left the bus carrying the cooler. Sam stood still in her position. As I got closer, I saw her eyes glistening, as if she'd either just finished or just begun crying.

"What are you doing out here?" I asked in my most innocent voice.

Sam wiped her eyes with her palms. "Just getting some air." She looked like she wanted to say something else, but didn't. She stood there, unmoving, and I did the same, like a gunfighter standoff in the center of town at high noon. At last, her body relaxed, and she reached out and took the cooler from me. "Come on, let's get in there. It's going to be a wild night."

Bozeman and I sat at a table off to the side and tried to stay out of the way while people funneled into the room. The ceremony was supposed to start at seven on the dot, and a check on my phone told me it was already a quarter after the appointed hour. Mayor Mary Sweets sat front and center, but the seats on either side of her were empty. She seemed to be an amiable woman, in her early sixties, dressed in a navy-blue business suit and a simple string of pearls. The mayor talked to everyone who approached her, shook their hands, and smiled graciously. I'm sure had there been any babies in the area, she would have given out kisses like they were going out of style. When there was no one near her, I could tell she wasn't happy with the situation. She kept checking her watch, and her body language screamed that she didn't like to be kept waiting.

Sam looked nervous. She paced beside the door, and as people entered, she greeted everyone, directed them to their seat, and went back to pacing.

Everyone I met earlier in the day seemed on edge as well, but as the bartenders opened the wine bottles and filled the glasses, a quiet calm settled over the crowd.

It was seven-thirty when Sherman Stier and his party strolled into the room. Sam ushered them to the front table and dismissed herself. Sherman introduced the rest of his party to the mayor, and they all sat.

Pastor Tom appeared from nowhere and took the stage. I saw him walking toward my microphone, so I jumped up and turned it on before he got there. He nodded his appreciation, and I retook my seat.

"Welcome everyone, please rise and join me for a quick prayer before we get started. Heavenly Father…"

Like everyone else, I stood and listened to the words, but although I bowed my head, I kept my eyes open and I scanned the room. Although most of the attendees prayed as expected, a few didn't. Lisa and Rob McMurtry were both standing at the back. Lisa stood behind a pushcart loaded with pitchers of water, iced teas, and soda, and Rob was holding back the wait staff. With the delay, I hoped people liked lukewarm food.

Hanson busily fussed with a flower display at the table in front of him, and for some odd reason, Dean Williams was staring directly at me.

"… Amen." Pastor Tom finished and invited everyone to sit. "Before the meals are served, I'd like to invite the mayor up to say a few words. Mayor Mary?"

To polite applause, the pastor took a step back to make room for the mayor on stage.

"Thank you, Pastor Tom, and thank you to everyone for attending. When the Main Street Committee first approached me to bring more business into our town, I admit I thought it would be a great goal, but also an ambitious one. You and I know our little corner of New Mexico offers a lot to travelers, but how do we get that word out to those passing by on the interstate? I was so excited when the committee came to me with a well thought out plan that could actually grow business. It's time to introduce that committee now and have them say a few words about what they've each been working on. I'll start with the chair, Mr. Sherman Stier."

Polite applause rang through the space again. As Sherman

walked to the stage, I glanced at Sam, who was in the process of an eye roll.

"Thank you, Mayor Mary." Sherman was taller than the microphone, and rather than adjust the stand higher, he bent over to make himself heard. "In any corporation, it's important to keep a close eye on the rock bottom line, which fosters well-being with the investors. It's no different from a town. Imagine yourself all as investors in this town and imagine that you have a sea of customers passing us daily, going seventy miles an hour right past us. If you want to bring them in, you need a purpose, and you have to give them either value or an experience, and I know we can do both. By building a top-notch golf course surrounded by a resort, we'll give travelers a reason to come here. To relax. To enjoy all the amenities that this great town offers. Together, we can build a future."

As Sherman took his seat, I leaned over to Bozeman. "I wonder where he was all day. Committee comes in and sets everything up, and the chair shows up late without contributing a single thing?"

"You never know. Maybe he fronted the costs and had important meetings to attend."

I shrugged. Bozeman was right. I didn't know the entire story, nor did I need to. I was just a gig player, and I had already gotten paid, so all we needed to do was sing a few songs, then head out to the next town.

The mayor introduced each committee member one at a time. They stepped up and told the audience what their specific actions were to drive business for the town. Each member focused on a specific area. Dean Williams was putting together a regional history tour. Its goal was to highlight the contributions of the town and county toward westward expansion. Reba Chestnut, the bed-and-breakfast owner, introduced her daughter, Robin. Robin was developing a nighttime haunted tour. The McMurtrys were creating a cookbook featuring local favorite recipes. Sam and Hanson had created a booklet that included many Quincey businesses that she intended to hand out at wedding planning events around the area.

"Of course, we can't do this all alone. We need your help," Mayor Mary said as a part of her closing statement. "Although we have a lot of great ideas already started, there is room for more. There's a table at the entrance with note cards. Please jot down any ideas you have and drop them in the box on the table. If you wish to remain anonymous, that's fine, and if you want to volunteer to serve the community, add your name and phone number. We have another presentation planned for later in the evening, but for now, I know you've been waiting to eat, so let's get down to dinner."

The mayor got the largest applause of the night at that remark, and she laughed as she took her seat. From the rear of the room, Rob guided the servers to tables with the meals as Lisa dashed from person to person to fill glasses.

"Well, I guess we're up," I said to Bozeman. I took a moment to tuck a stray strand of hair under my hat and took my place at the microphone. "Hey everyone, my name is Codi Cassidy, and this is Bozeman James. Thank you for having us, and we hope you enjoy your dinner."

I gave Bozeman a nod, and we launched into our set. Since we were playing over dinner, we did an entire acoustic set without the backing tracks. As usual, people focused on the food and those around them rather than us. Sam could've hired a DJ or turned on a radio as background music, but I was still thankful she thought enough of me to book us for the gig. This part was the dinner. The after-dinner set was the one where we'd let loose and have fun.

After twenty minutes of tunes, I announced we were taking a break and Bozeman and I made our way to a table in the back. Within a couple minutes of sitting, Rob dropped off plates of food for us. It was standard event fare. Baked chicken, mashed potatoes and gravy, corn, and a dinner roll I recognized as one of Sam's. My stomach rumbled the second I picked up my fork. I was ready to dig in. Bozeman was already at it.

"That was pretty good. Are you going to play your hit song?" Rob asked as he stepped back.

"I usually save that one for the encore. Since we're not doing an encore tonight, it'll be the last song of the set."

"I have to wait that long?" Rob frowned, and his shoulders shrugged like a five-year-old being told they couldn't have a cookie.

"Of course. We have to give the audience something to look forward to. Don't want to play the big hit first, then have a bunch of people leave because they got what they came for."

"I guess that makes sense," Rob said.

"Oh, I've got an autographed photo for you. It's up there on the piano. Come pick it up after the show, okay?"

Rob's body language shifted in a moment, and he was upbeat and looked happy again. "I'll be back in a moment with some pie." I wished all my fans were so easy to please and were so quick to offer me pie.

Bozeman had cleaned his plate before I had eaten half of my meal.

"You not liking that?" Bozeman asked.

"Love it. I'm just waiting for dessert." I put my fork beside the plate and glanced at Bozeman. Based on the way he stared at my unfinished meal, I could tell he was still hungry. "Go ahead," I said.

Bozeman reached for my plate. At the last second, I snatched my dinner roll back and took a bite. It, like the muffin, was heavenly. I had just finished the roll when Rob reappeared and slid slices of Dutch apple pie before us. With eager anticipation, I slid my fork through the pie and took a bite. The crust was flaky, and the sweet crumble on top was the perfect complement to the tart apples inside. I moaned as I chewed and the flavors exploded, and I glanced at Bozeman, who had almost finished with his slice already.

Bozeman scraped the fork side against the plate's bottom to

get the remaining crumbs, ate it, and sat back. "I think I want to marry Sam."

I took a drink of water and smiled at him. "Silly man. I've known her longer, so she's mine. Don't worry though, I'll throw scraps out the back door to you."

Bozeman grinned. "Even better."

I finished my pie and looked toward the stage where the committee was still doing post-dinner presentations. As I sighed, I hoped the talking would be over soon. I was itching to play, and I was already thinking about getting on the road over to the next gig. I knew my mind shouldn't wander, but it often did during downtimes like these.

Bozeman nudged me in the ribs to knock me from my daydreaming and pointed to the stage, where Sam stood waving, trying to get my attention. I adjusted my hat, and we took to the stage for our second set. I grabbed my guitar and checked the computer while Bozeman made sure he switched all the electronics on. Then suddenly, it was showtime. We buzzed through a few country standards, a few modern songs, and slid in a couple of originals as well. The set was going swimmingly. I saw the audience was engaged, and they moved a few of the tables closest to the stage to create a dance floor. The chords were tight, and the sound was brilliant. From a performer's standpoint, it was a great show.

They pushed aside more tables when we played a number suitable for a Texas two-step. As I looked into the crowd, I estimated that many of the original two hundred people that were there for dinner had stayed for the show. There was the usual percentage of folks who didn't dance and would either listen to the music or chat with friends, but that was fine by me. I also noticed at one point, every member of the committee gathered near the back door and clustered in a tight circle. Sherman noticed it as well, so he broke off the side conversation with Mayor Mary and headed in a beeline for the group, pushing aside anyone who got into his path. From my position on the stage, he looked like a bull chasing a matador.

Hanson saw Sherman coming and must have informed the group because most of them turned and looked. With the rest of the circle distracted by the oncoming problem, Hanson silently slipped out the service door. Lisa, who was standing next to Hanson, followed him out the door. Since I was in the middle of a Willie Nelson tune, I couldn't stop playing. Over the din, I also couldn't determine what they were discussing. I saw Sherman was using animated gestures wild enough to cause Sam and Rob, who were standing on either side of him, to take a step back.

I glanced at Bozeman to see if he saw the same thing I did. As I followed his sight line, it appeared he was more interested in a buxom brunette in a yellow sundress who was swaying in front of the stage.

I redirected my vision to the rear of the room and saw Sherman shove Sam. Sherman raised his hand and balled his fist, and Sam shrank to the ground. With great haste, Rob stepped in and grabbed Sherman's arm before Sherman could strike. Sherman tried to pull himself free but couldn't. Reba escorted Sam from the room while Rob and Dean held Sherman back from pursuing her. Rob and Dean held Sherman for a full minute, then Sherman put up his hands in surrender and the men let him go. Dean rushed from the room, Sherman started pacing back and forth, and Rob came forward to find the mayor.

Mayor Mary was in the center of the dance floor being spun around by a cowboy when Rob cut in. Rather than dance, Rob leaned in and whispered something in her ear. She said something back I couldn't hear. Rob nodded, and they both left the room through the main door. I finished the song, then grabbed my water bottle to take a drink as I looked again at the back. Sherman was gone.

I stepped aside and let Bozeman sing a couple of his originals, then I took the lead again. I was ready to begin my big single when I saw the mayor return to the room, followed by the town's police chief. Close behind the steps of the chief was a deputy. In the back of the room, the committee filed back into the room, followed by another deputy.

The chief stepped onto the stage and tipped his hat at me. "Sorry, ma'am. I need to interrupt the show."

I took a couple of steps to the right, and he took my place in front of the mic. "Attention everyone. There's been an incident, and we ask everyone here to sit tight until you're questioned by myself or a deputy. As soon as we get your contact information, you're free to leave unless we ask you to stay. When you go, exit from the side door only. For now, please find a seat and be patient with us. Thank you."

"What's going on?" I asked.

The chief took off his hat and ran a handkerchief across his brow. "Someone murdered Sherman Stier."

CHAPTER FIVE

The concert came to an abrupt end, and not in the usual cheerful way. Although the chief wouldn't allow us to leave, he granted Bozeman and me permission to pack up our gear. I assumed the chief had us included in the suspect pool simply by being in the building at the time of the murder, but I didn't fret about it. Being on stage in front of a few hundred people was always an iron-clad alibi. Well, not always, but that's a different story.

I was shutting down the laptop and disconnecting its cables when I felt a tap on the shoulder. I did a quick pivot, expecting Rob wanting his autographed picture. Instead, when I turned, Sam stood there.

"Are you okay, Sam?" She didn't look okay. Her face appeared pale, her hair looked messy, and her frown almost extended down to her shoulders. She still carried the sparkle in her eyes, but even it seemed muted.

"Codi, I… I think I'm in big trouble."

"What? Why? Come over here and sit down." I pulled out the piano bench and Sam took a hesitant step forward and sat down. She looked down at her feet and refused to look up at me.

Sam's eyes watered and she quietly began crying. Instinctively, I reached out to pat her on the shoulder, then noticed her shirt had little dark red dots over the front of it. I pulled my hand away.

"Sam, why is there blood on your shirt?"

She didn't answer right away. I looked into the room. Several law enforcement officers were collecting contact information from the guests. Way in the back, they had the committee sequestered to a few tables. Rob, Dean, and Hanson huddled in a tight circle talking to each other. Reba worked on drinking a bottle of wine, seemingly by herself. Her indulgence was probably against advice, considering how she looked around the room anytime she refilled her glass. Pastor Tom ministered to Lisa, who seemed to be in the middle of a full-on breakdown. Shanna sat off to the side, not talking to anyone. I hadn't even known she was at the event, but based on the apron and hairnet she wore, I guessed she had been a part of the kitchen staff for the evening.

Sam showed no signs of slowing down, so I left her for a moment to round up a handful of napkins. When I returned, she took the napkins and dried her eyes. I sat patiently by her side and waited for her to compose herself. I estimated the number of people in the room and guessed it would be at least an hour before I would go anywhere.

After a few minutes, she finally stopped crying, dried her eyes for a last time, and blew her nose. She looked around for somewhere to put her used napkins, and finding none, she balled them up and stuffed them into the front pocket of her jeans.

"Thanks. I needed that," Sam said. Her voice, still quiet, sounded stronger.

"Sam, what's going on?" I asked.

"Codi, I didn't do it. I didn't kill him."

"I believe you." Then again, what was I going to say? I didn't honestly know if she had done it or not. It's hard to be a witness for people if they're not in the same room as you. Besides, her shirt looked like a Jackson Pollock painting.

"Sam. Talk to me. What happened?"

Sam looked up for a brief second, then down at the floor. "We had some words. He's been trying to rattle my cage for over a month, trying to force me to sell my bakery, and tonight he did it again. I called him a jerk, and he pushed me, and we moved into the kitchen. The next thing I know, he's dead. Please believe me. I didn't do it."

"All you did was call him a name, and he pushed you for that?" I asked.

Sam nodded.

I'm not sure if I accepted that or not. In my line of work, I've seen my share of tough men. But usually, the rich ones seemed a little more careful about displaying random acts of violence, especially in a room filled with witnesses. If something set Sherman off, I doubt if it was being called a jerk. After all, there are a lot of worse things to be called. But again, I didn't know him, either. He might be one of those guys who flew off the handle at the least bit of provocation.

"The police are here. They can help you," I said.

"No. It has to be you. You can do it. Remember back at Greenway High when the school mascot got stolen, and you found him and figured out who kidnapped him?"

That brought back memories. I made the front page of the school newspaper and page five of the *Denver Post* local section when I cracked that mystery. It brought a smile as I remembered how proud my dad was of me. It was the first adventure of Codi Cassidy, Girl Detective.

Someone had sheep-napped Ramsey the Ram the week before homecoming. The Denver police were called in, but since the theft of a single animal didn't rank high on their priority list, school security had to take the lead. Of course, all eyes were on our rivals for the big game, Henry Teller High, but that was a little too on the nose for me. I asked around, followed a few leads, and eventually fingered the true culprits, a couple of bad kids who had gotten expelled the year before. By the time kickoff came around, Ramsey was back on the sidelines in his blue and gold blanket, chomping away at his fresh hay. The return of the sacred mascot didn't help, though, the football team still lost the game by thirty-five points.

What started as a mission to impress my father turned out to be a bane of my existence. For the rest of the school year, my classmates wanted me to track down missing items and pets like I was the cowgirl version of Nancy Drew. I didn't get involved in another case until much later, and that's another story, too.

I looked Sam in the eyes. "Sam, I'll say it again. I'm not a cop, I'm a musician, I don't see what I can do to help. Even if I did, I wouldn't know how to investigate a death. I've never even seen a dead person outside of a funeral home."

"But you're good with people. They open up to you. Please, ask around and see if anyone else noticed anything."

I was about to respond when the chief approached. He looked way too young to be the chief of police, but based on the nameplate on his shirt, that's who he was. The chief looked sixteen, but I assumed he had to be in his late thirties. He had reddish-brown hair clipped short, freckles on his nose, and a scowl on his face he must have developed over a lifetime of bullying people younger than him. I admonished myself for judging a book by its cover, so I smiled, put my hand out and stepped forward to introduce myself.

He stepped past me like I wasn't there and got right into Sam's face.

"Ma'am, please, I asked you not to talk to anyone. Find a spot to sit down and stay quiet. I don't want to put you in handcuffs."

Sam took a step backward; I took a step forward. "Can she at least change out of that shirt?" I asked.

The chief finally noticed me and looked at Sam, considered it for a moment, and nodded. "I would prefer to collect the evidence at the station, but I don't want you spreading it all over the room, either. You got something to change into?"

Sam shook her head. "Of course not."

"Here, I have a fresh shirt for you." I stepped off the stage and found the plastic tote we stored our merchandise in. I rooted around in there until I found a shirt for her. "You look like a medium, but I only have large. Will that do? And I've got a bag here that you can put the dirty one in."

Sam took the shirt and moved to step off the stage.

"Where are you going?" the chief asked.

"To the ladies' room to change."

The look in the chief's eye said everything, and Sam stopped in her tracks. "You need to change here, or not at all. Can't have you destroying evidence," he said.

Did I detect a slight smile curl up on his lips like a cartoon villain? Must have been a trick of the light, or the perception of the man I was building in my head.

"Fine." Sam stepped back onto the stage, turned so her back was facing us, and started taking off her shirt. To Bozeman's credit, he stepped in front of her and shielded her as best he could with his enormous frame. I was only a couple feet away, and I caught no glimpse of flesh during her quick change. A couple of seconds later, Sam turned back around, displaying my face on her chest. It was by far my favorite photo. Head back, wide smile, hand holding my hat on my head. She stuffed the soiled shirt into the plastic bag I handed her and passed the bag to the chief.

"Don't go anywhere, Sam. I mean it." The chief took the bag from her outstretched hand, knotted the top, then returned to his business.

"What's his deal? He doesn't seem to like you much," I said as I closed up the merchandise bin.

Sam took in a breath of air, then released it with a sigh. "I expect that's because he's asked me out a few times and I've always turned him down."

"Wait, you know him?" I asked.

"Of course. It's a small town. Everyone knows everyone. He comes into the bakery two or three times a week."

"And he's asked you out?"

"Yes. Like out for dinner, or to the movies, like a date," Sam said. The shirt I'd given her was too big, so she tucked it into her jeans.

"You've always said no?"

"Of course. I'm not really interested in seeing anyone right now. I'm still getting over my last breakup, so I've been throwing myself into my baking. Besides, he's not my type. I've heard rumors he can be… really mean. So please. Will you help me?"

I didn't know what to think. On the one hand, I had no business getting myself involved. On the other hand, I also had no business getting involved, but I had a desire to jump in anyway. The police were here, and they'd figure it out. All I had to do was pack up my gear, wait for my turn to be interviewed, and then ride off into the sunset like a good little cowgirl. I glanced at Bozeman, even though I already guessed where he stood. He shook his head, turned, and started coiling a microphone cable.

"Look, I can't make any promises. You can understand that, right?"

Sam smiled for the first time since she approached me. "Yes, of course."

"You expect people will talk to me? I am an outsider, after all. Not everyone will be an open book for me."

"Yeah, but they realize you're my friend, so you have that connection. Besides, you're a star. People always want to hang out with a star."

The term star was a little generous, considering I never played the Grand Ole Opry, but I understood what she meant. Most people enjoyed getting attention from the performers, which could be a benefit or a curse, depending on the situation. I admit, I've gotten better service at restaurants occasionally. And I once got upgraded from coach class to business class on a flight just because the gate agent liked my second album. A lot of times I let people down, regardless of how many autographs I give out or selfies I take with people. Most fans are great and only want to shake my hand and say hello, but sometimes people get a little too fanatical. On more than one occasion, Bozeman, or the venue security has had to rescue me from an eager fan who wanted to monopolize my time.

"I can't offer any promises," I said sternly.

"You said that already."

"I just wanted to make it clear. I'm way out of my element here." Out of my element was an understatement.

I couldn't stand the sad, hound dog eyes Sam was giving to me. "Okay, fine. But first, tell me how it was you came to have a shirt covered in blood? Tell me what happened. Leave nothing out."

"Like I said, I called Sherman a name, and he pushed me. After that, I went out the back door into the kitchen to cool off because I didn't want to make a scene."

"Stop. Back up. Why did you call him out in the first place? What precipitated that?"

"He must have had too much wine tonight because every time he was near, he'd give me a crack about losing my bakery. Or how he was going to own me, or how I'd be begging him for a job. Then, to top it off, he pinched me on the rear."

"He didn't," I said.

"He did," Sam confirmed.

"Anyone observe that?"

"I can't be sure. There was already a crowd of people around, and it happened so fast. That's when I turned around and called him a jerk. Then he pushed me, and rather than take it any further, I left the room," Sam said.

"Anyone see you?"

"Of course. Reba was right on my tail, and Shanna and some other folks were in the kitchen. They all saw me."

"Then what happened?"

"Well, Reba suggested I go to the restroom to wash my face, so I did. I stayed in there for perhaps five or six minutes, then came out."

"And then?" I asked.

"Well, then I ran into Dean."

"What do you mean by ran into him?" I asked.

"Just as I stepped out of the restroom, Dean was right there, as if he were waiting for me. He was angry that Sherman had pushed me."

"Did he say anything?"

"He was mostly just doing what I call his rattle. He gets all worked up to the point where he can't verbalize a single thought. The only clear thing I got from him was he said he couldn't believe Sherman had done that. Then he stomped off. I think he left the church to get some air. Walking around is his way of calming down. I swear, the man must put in thirty miles a day."

I hated to ask the next question, because I didn't quite get how to put it, so I said it as simply as I could. "Are you two... involved?"

She looked at me as if the words I said were in Arabic instead of English. I was thinking of a less subtle way to ask if they were spending quality time between the sheets together when things clicked for her, and she laughed at me.

"Oh, no. I dated him briefly, but we broke it off. We weren't compatible as a couple. I don't like him that way."

"Does he understand you're not a couple? Based on his body language alone, I'd say you two are the hottest item in town."

Sam blushed. "No. We're just... good friends. Dean is over-protective of me, and gets jealous sometimes, even though we're not together. That's one of the many reasons I couldn't get into a relationship with him. He has this old-fashioned way of thinking about what a woman is supposed to be, and I'm the opposite of that. He sees me as a stay at home, raise the children, and bake cakes type of woman who wears dresses and brings him a martini when he comes home at night. I'm the complete opposite of that. I enjoy being my independent self, and I don't feel like I need to be in any relationship where I can't be the person who I want to be."

Unfortunately, I wasn't sure she was telling me the whole truth, but for the time being, her relationships didn't enter the equation. "Go on. What went on after Dean left?"

"I headed back to the kitchen. I had stepped part way down the hall when I noticed the pantry door was ajar."

In my mind, I pictured the pantry on my bus, which spans from roof to floor, but is only a whopping twelve inches wide. "What type of pantry?"

"The church calls it the pantry, but it's only your average storeroom. It's used to hold the food donations they get for the giving box out front. It's also where they store the equipment that won't fit in the kitchen. Anyway, the door was open, so I wondered if anyone was in there. I tried to open the door wider, but something was blocking it from the other side. I pushed against it really hard, and finally it gave way, threw me off balance, and I fell in. When I did, I landed… by Sherman. And when I tried to get up, I slipped and ended up with my shirt a mess."

I nodded. Seemed plausible. Barely. "Anything else?"

"I had just regained my footing and was going to get help when Shanna popped in and started screaming. Within the next couple of minutes, people surrounded me, and they held me until the police got here."

I didn't really want to learn the in-depth forensic details, but there was one thing I needed to get. "How was he killed?"

Sam glanced at me, then stared at her feet. Never a good sign. "He… he got stabbed in the stomach."

I learned from experience, more my father's than my own, that getting stabbed in the abdomen wasn't always a death sentence. Unless the stabber nicked a vital organ or major artery. "Are you sure he was dead?"

"I don't know. After I fell and saw him, I freaked out. All I wanted to do was get out of there, so I didn't check."

"Could you tell if he was breathing?" I asked.

"I'm telling you, I don't know. Heavens, I'm a baker, not a doctor."

Sam's tone dropped, and the way she punctuated her words made her sound defensive. I stayed silent for a good two minutes, waiting to see if she'd offer any additional information, but she didn't.

"Did you hear if anyone called for an ambulance?" I thought by moving away from asking about her, she'd warm back up to me.

She stopped for a moment, as if trying to recall the memory. "I don't know. I noticed Ty was there pretty quick, but I only saw him briefly entering the room as I was being held outside."

After thinking for a moment, I didn't recall being introduced to a Ty. "Who's he?"

"He's the paramedic that runs with the volunteer fire department. Must have been his shift off, because he was here at the event, although he spent most of his time in the kitchen with his girlfriend, Bethany."

I made a mental note to reach out to Ty later. If he hadn't already taken off with the victim.

"So other than Dean and Shanna, you didn't see anyone else around when you found Sherman?"

Sam stayed silent for a moment. I could see her wheels turning. She shook her head. "No. I didn't see anyone. Although I could hear other people, which wasn't a surprise since the kitchen was just another few steps down the hall."

Sam stopped speaking, and I waited for her to fill in any other blanks voluntarily, but she didn't. At last, she looked me directly in the eyes.

"I'm in deep trouble, aren't I?"

I didn't quite know how to respond. It sure seemed like it to me. "I hope not, Sam."

I glanced up and saw the chief was charging to the stage like a man on a mission. He must've been watching us, because without a word, he took Sam by the arm and led her across the room and out the back door. I hoped he was taking her to the kitchen and not the police station, but I didn't desire to run after them and check.

Bozeman carried a microphone stand past me, folded it up, and set it on the floor.

"Bozeman, how long will it take us to get to Los Angeles?"

"Oh, ten or eleven hours, depending on stops and traffic."

"We have nothing planned on route, do we?" I asked. Sometimes we stopped off for touristy things, like a visit to the Grand Canyon. At other times we liked to visit friends or industry people while we were on the road.

"Nothing in concrete. We could drive it straight through if we had to. Are you thinking about staying around for another day or two?"

"Perhaps."

"You believe her entire story?" Bozeman asked.

I wanted to ask how much he heard, but I guessed it had to be the whole thing. Although he wasn't much of a talker, he was an excellent listener, even when he didn't mean to be. How much was believable? That's what it came down to. The stories people told could be one hundred percent solid truth. Or one hundred percent solid bat guano, and I suspect that Sam's tale lay somewhere in the middle, but hopefully more toward the truth end.

"There were a few parts in there I wondered about," I said.

"Yeah. Me too," Bozeman said.

"Although I guess I'll never find the full truth unless I seek it out."

CHAPTER SIX

In my head, I laid out a plan of attack, and then I scanned the room ahead of me. Since the committee had been involved in the circle of confrontation earlier, they composed the people I wanted to speak to first. Hopefully, they'd succumb to my charms and be open to discussion. Otherwise, it would be a night of quick conversations. It was just a matter of whom to approach first. It didn't take long to make my decision.

Reba had worked her way through almost an entire bottle of Sauvignon Blanc by the time I took a seat across from her. She let out a little yelp, as if it surprised her that anyone in a room filled with people would join her. She pulled the bottle closer to her, subconsciously telling me it was all hers and I'd have to get my own.

Reba gestured at me with the glass in her hand. "Do you always have blue hair?" I watched the wine climb three quarters of the way up the glass, then descend again.

"Not always, but for now. I like to switch it up. Blue, green, orange, white, black. All depends on my mood when I decide it needs a change," I said.

"Why? Why not keep your own color?" I'm glad I talked to Reba first. Her cheeks looked a tinge redder than when I met her earlier, and she was already slurring her words. I felt lucky to catch her before she nodded off into a grape-induced slumber for the evening.

"Want to hear a secret?" I asked.

Reba and I leaned in toward each other like we were girls gossiping in math class.

"I started going gray in my early twenties, so I started dying it blonde, but then I branched out to other colors when I got bored with the blonde."

Reba sat back, took a drink, then scoffed at me. "You think that's a secret? That's not a secret. You want to tell a secret, it has to be a juicy one. I got lots of secrets. I've been in this town for eighty years, and I know where they buried all those bodies."

Reba hadn't struck me as the town busybody when I met her, but I realized she could be helpful to me. If she stayed awake and coherent, that was.

I leaned across the table even further. "Oh my. Tell me a secret then. A juicy one."

Reba looked from side to side, then took a quick glance behind her to see if anyone was listening in. "Kayla's pregnant, and although Lionel thinks he's the father, he's not. And get this, Stevie, down at the farm store? He's cheating on his wife *and* on his taxes." Reba produced a wide grin, then sat back and outstretched her arms with her palms up. All she was missing was the hat and wand to make it a true magic trick.

It wasn't quite what I was looking for, but it was a start. I returned her grin in kind. "Wow. That's some dirt!"

Reba took another swig, then turned serious. "Oh, trust me, I have enough dirt to bury this entire town."

"I'll bet you do. You must have lots of secrets about the committee." It was a little pointed, but I felt I needed to direct the conversation, since I didn't really care who was having whose baby.

"Sure. Have you met Hanson, the florist?"

I nodded. "Yes, we've met."

"He likes to pretend he's gay, but he's not. He's dating a schoolteacher in the next town over."

Not what I was looking for, but I played along. "Why would he pretend to be gay?"

"Because the idiot assumes he'll sell more flowers that way. He's the only flower shop in the county. His brother owns the Quincey Inn. His brother, Harold, tells me Hanson's an idiot too. Hanson thinks his affair with that math teacher is such a big secret, but everyone knows." Reba thought that was hilarious and cackled like a witch over a cauldron.

I struggled to smile in response. "Affair? You said dating."

"I used dating as a loose term, dear. He met that teacher on one of those affair websites. She's as married as the day is long. Rumor has it she's related to Sherman Stier. A niece or cousin, or something. Can you believe that?"

That was a juicy tidbit. I tucked that one away for later.

"You know the diner's going to go under." Reba blurted it out so fast on the heels of the Hanson rumors, I barely had a moment to adjust to the topic change.

"No way. I ate there last night, and not a seat was open. The food was delicious, too."

"True enough. The word is that the resort is locking in exclusive contracts with all the local meat and produce vendors. Can you imagine what that would do to the diner? I guess they wouldn't last for more than a month if that happened."

I didn't have to imagine. Either the diner would need to ship in supplies from far away, find new vendors, or close the doors. Since Quincey was in such a remote part of the state, it wasn't a tough guess to determine the outcome.

"Wouldn't that be the same for Sam's bakery? If the resort got exclusive vendor contracts, wouldn't she lose out too?" I asked.

Reba considered the point. "I guess so, but I don't know for sure. Want some wine?"

I shook my head. I wasn't much of a drinker anymore. "No thanks, but you go ahead."

Reba refilled her glass with the bottle's dregs. Her eyes looked red. I suspected it would be game over for her soon.

"You hear of anyone here with a grudge against Sherman?"

She shot me a sly glance. "You mean, like a killing grudge?"

I nodded.

"Sweetie, take a peek around. Sherman Stier has either stabbed or threatened to stab everyone here in the back. I swear, he lives to screw people over. He wants to buy up the entire downtown area. Wants to turn the museum into a bowling alley, I'm told. He wants my B&B out of business. He even wants to close the local golf course because it would compete with his new one. Can you imagine that? The local course is only nine holes, and it's full of cactus and sagebrush. Also, there's some hold he has on the mayor, but that's one secret I haven't been able to crack. I'd say the only one who wouldn't want him dead is good Pastor Tom, and that's only because he's a decent man of God."

Reba drained her glass. "I wonder how long they're going to keep us here." She closed her eyes and slipped off to sleep without another word.

"She's nutty, you know."

I looked over at the next table. Shanna was there, scrolling through whatever on her smart phone.

I let Reba sleep and switched tables. "You caught all that?"

Shanna shrugged. "Didn't mean to. She's just… too loud. She gets that way when she's had too much to drink. Exactly like you saw her. She drinks, gets talkative and loud, then passes out."

"What will happen to her?" I asked.

Shanna shrugged again. I took it as a personal tic. "Tom or Hanson, or perhaps Dean will get her back to the B and B and she'll wake up on her couch tomorrow morning and do it all over again."

"It's terrible what happened here, isn't it?"

"No. Not really."

Shanna's blunt response surprised me. I'll admit it. "Why not?"

Shanna stopped scrolling and set her phone on the table. "Because. Sometimes, and by sometimes, I mean rarely, bad people get what they deserve."

I was speechless. Was this the same Shanna from earlier who gave me my muffin and, I guessed, could be the sweetest woman in the world? "Why do you say that?"

"He's been pushing people in this town around since he got here. Throwing around money, making threats to close businesses down. Reba was right about one thing. He's got something on the mayor for sure. I've overheard the committee and others around town have been to her with complaints either about the man or that resort, and she has done nothing about it. A rumor that Reba didn't tell you is that the mayor will be in the political fight of her life when the next election cycle starts."

"Why?" I asked.

"Because she won't be running unopposed for once. I have to use the restroom."

Shanna picked up her phone as she stood and started for the door.

"Wait, who's running against her?"

She hesitated after a step, turned, and grinned. "Sam's boyfriend. Dean Williams."

I wanted to talk to Dean next, especially since Sam told me they weren't dating. When I finally spotted him, he was deep in conversation with Rob and Lisa, and I had no desire to intrude on the conversation. I really wanted to get him alone. Instead, I scanned the room. Besides the committee, there appeared to be around seventy-five people waiting to get interviewed by the police. By body language alone, I deduced most of them were itching to leave. My window of opportunity was closing. Fast.

I spotted Hanson near the stage. He was keeping busy by

collecting the centerpieces he provided and placing them on a single table near the front door. I grabbed the one in the center of my table and grabbed the one from the table where Reba was currently napping, and carried them to Hanson.

I set them down on the table with the others. "These are really lovely. Can I help you collect the others?"

Hanson took a step back and almost tripped over a chair, but he quickly regained his balance.

I grabbed his arm to help him. "Hey, I'm so sorry. I didn't mean to startle you."

Hanson smiled. "That's okay. I got lost in my thoughts. What were you saying?"

"I said I like these centerpieces. They're pretty."

Hanson looked at the growing number of them on the table. "Oh. Thank you. They're nothing special. Carnations and daisies and whatnot. We didn't have a large budget for flowers."

"What are you going to do with them?"

Hanson blinked twice. I wasn't sure if he was all there or not.

"Usually people will take them, but I suppose with the… distraction, most of them are being left behind. I'll probably recycle the materials and the flowers will end up in the mulch pile."

"That's so sad something so beautiful will end up as mulch."

Hanson shrugged. "That's the nature of this business. Some flowers get dried and saved, or pressed into scrapbooks, but I'd say ninety-eight percent of them go into the trash."

"That's terrible. You'd assume they would donate them to a church, or a cemetery, or something."

"That occurs more often than not. Especially around the bigger holidays like Christmas, Easter, and Valentine's Day. But then what does the church and cemetery do with them when they've wilted away?"

I got the picture. "They end up on the mulch pile."

"Or in the town dump. Not a very romantic end, is it? It's the tragic irony of my business. People want to give flowers as a symbol of love and beauty, but the moment the flowers are picked is the second they start to wither and die."

"I never considered that." It was true, I hadn't. Although, to be honest, I've given flowers to no one, and I haven't received one since my corsage for senior prom.

"I saw you over there talking to Reba. Did she spin any wonderful tales for you?"

"You mean about your affair?" I said to myself. But I had the sense not to verbalize that. "She mentioned your brother owns the Quincey Inn. That's pretty cool. I read that historical plaque on the building when I passed by it yesterday. It seems like an interesting place. I'd like to go in and see it before I leave town."

Hanson gave me a look that told me he picked up what I laid down and was avoiding the topic.

"He's only a part-owner. I'm sure he owns fifty or sixty percent of the hotel, but you'd have to ask him."

"I don't recall meeting him. Is he here tonight? I thought he's on the committee."

Hanson wiped his brow on his sleeve and sat. "He's not in town. He's back in Taos with our parents. My dad broke a leg when he fell off a ladder, so Harold's up there helping mom take care of him."

"That's nice of him. You didn't go too?"

Hanson shook his head no. "No need for both of us. It's easier for him to get away. He's got an entire staff to run the hotel in his absence, so it's not uncommon for him to be away. Me, I've only got one assistant, and she's in junior college full time, so I have to run the flower shop mostly on my own. I would've loved to run home for a month or two, but that would have meant shutting the doors until I returned."

Made sense. I didn't detect any animosity between him and his brother. Well, maybe a small twinge of jealousy, and I could understand that.

"How did you get into the floral industry?" I asked.

Hanson rolled his eyes. "Actually, I wanted to be a mechanic, but I hated coming home every night dirty and smelling like grease. It was my mom's flower shop, so when she started talking about retiring, I became her apprentice and took over the place. So, Kelly, what is it you really need from me?"

I guessed the gig was up. "Codi. Not Kelly. I've learned from a couple of people that Sherman Stier had a lot of enemies in this town."

"Thanks for your honesty, Codi. That can be a hard thing to find around here." Hanson used a foot to shove a chair toward me, and I sat. "I try to keep my nose on my face and not in other people's business, you understand, so I won't tell you much. I'll tell you what I'm going to tell the cops if I ever get my turn. Yes, there was a lot of bad blood between him and a lot of folks here. No, I can't guess who he pushed to the breaking point."

"What about the argument you all were having earlier? What was that about?"

Hanson became interested in a fingernail and started picking at a cuticle. "Dean wanted us to approach the mayor tonight as a group, so maybe she'd finally do something about Stier."

"What resulted from that?" I asked.

Hanson forgot about his finger and paid more attention to me. "Beats me. I didn't want to get involved, so I slipped out of the back door and headed to the kitchen."

"What for?"

"To see if I could scrounge up another slice of pie and talk to some ladies."

"What happened?"

"Like I said, I had some pie, and talked to one lovely volunteer washing the dishes."

I went for the jugular. "Your girlfriend wouldn't object to that?"

Hanson looked a bit taken, then stood. "Nice talking to you, Kelly. Make sure you take a centerpiece with you when you leave."

Hanson walked away without looking back. Information-wise, he was a bust.

I grunted, hopefully loud enough for him to hear. "It's Codi."

I glanced up and saw Dean was sitting alone, nursing a bottle of soda. He saw me coming, looked for a place to escape to, and finding no safe passage, stayed where he was.

"Howdy," I said as I approached him.

He stared at me as if he didn't speak Texan. Dean took a swig of his soda and went to work peeling the label from the plastic bottle.

"You don't seem to like me much. Why not?" I asked.

His brow furrowed. "Mama said never to trust outsiders, and never to trust girls with guitars, and especially never to trust outsider girls with guitars."

I threw him my best smile. "That's sound advice. Your mama is a smart woman."

Dean scowled. "What are you here for?"

"I came to town to sing my songs and entertain y'all." I assumed that was self-explanatory, considering I'd spent most of the evening on the stage doing just that.

"No. I meant, what are you here for right now? I saw you sniffing around the others. What do you want from me?"

"Let me shoot it straight, slugger. Sam's a friend. We go way, way back, and she's about to find herself in a whole heap of trouble. I want to help her avoid that if I can. Can you tell me what went on earlier tonight?"

"I don't get what you mean." Dean set his soda on the table and crossed his arms. This wasn't going the way I expected or wanted it to.

"I saw the pow-wow y'all were having in the back, and I saw Sherman shove Sam."

Dean threw his left leg over his right. He was going into full shutdown mode. If there was a box or closet handy, I felt certain he'd go right for it.

"Well?" I asked.

Dean just pursed his lips tight and blew. I bet if I put a trumpet before him, he could perform *The Flight of the Bumblebee* with little effort. Perhaps I needed to change my line of questioning.

"I understand you and Sam are seeing each other. If you're sweet on each other, then for sure you'd want to help her, right? That's what I'm trying to do. Help her. Can't you help me? Do what's best for Sam?"

Had his eyes been lasers, he would have drilled a hole right through my forehead.

"Do you know why Sherman shoved Sam, and what happened afterward?"

Dean dropped his foot to the floor, put his elbow on his knee, and rested his chin on his elbow. He could have modeled for Rodan's *Thinker* if the statue was based on rage instead of logic.

"Can you tell me anything at all? Please? For Sam's sake?"

Dean's ears turned from pink to red, and I suspected there was an internal volcano churning inside him. I'd seen enough confrontations throughout my career to recognize when one was on the way. It was time to take my leave while the time was at hand.

"Okay. I'll go. But if you want to talk, I'll be around for a while longer. Think about Sam. Think about what she'd want you to do."

I left Dean stewing in his juices and looked across the room to see who else might have any helpful information.

I also needed to talk to Sam again and find out why she lied to me.

Looking around, I figured the pool of people I wanted to interview had reduced to about half, although I'd love another shot at Dean. I suspected he was hiding something behind that brick wall he threw up. Was it something to do with Sam? Was it something to do with a murder? I didn't know. One thing I knew for sure was I had to use the facilities, and since those were in the same hallway as the pantry, I hoped to get a look at that, too. I'm not a trained criminologist, but I figured I might spot something that the police overlooked. Like perhaps a signed confession, or the crime captured on video.

I walked through the room to the back door and turned right, which led me into the kitchen. The kitchen was empty, and I assumed that everyone who worked in there during the event had gone into the gymnasium. I turned around and walked down the hall. It only took a few strides to get to the pantry. The door was closed, and there was a giant X marked off in yellow crime scene tape. I wanted to open the door and look anyway, but when I reached for the doorknob, I noticed they covered it with fingerprint dust. I didn't want to add to that mess, nor did I want to be covered with dust, so I gave up that quest for the moment.

The restroom was just down the hall from the pantry, just like Sam had said. There wasn't much to the ladies' room. It was small. Three stalls and two sinks, and I was lucky enough to have the entire thing to myself. I selected the far stall and took care of business. It was good to be alone for a few minutes, and I soaked up the quiet like a sunflower basking in the sunlight. I closed my eyes for a moment and took a few cleansing breaths.

"I don't think Sam did it, even though everyone is saying she did." In the small room, the voice echoed over every fixture and shattered my moment of serenity.

"Are you talking to me?" I asked.

"Of course. We're the only two in here. C'mon out of there."

I got myself together, slid the lock open, and left the stall. Lisa stood at a sink. She was busy staring into the mirror and fixing her hair. I approached the remaining sink and washed my hands.

"Why does everyone assume she's guilty?" I took my time

rinsing my hands. The water felt warm and relaxing, but I couldn't stay under there forever, so I shut off the tap and reached for the paper towels.

Satisfied with her look, Lisa turned from the mirror and looked at me. "Lots of reasons. They've been at each other's throats since they met. Sherman wanted to buy her out and close the bakery."

"I have firsthand knowledge of that. I was at the bakery earlier when he came in with a group of other men."

Lisa interrupted. "Investors from the city. Sherman doesn't… didn't have enough of his own money for everything he wanted, so he started bringing in investors about a year ago."

"He offered her a job at the new resort." I threw the used towels into the trash can.

Lisa laughed at that. "Oh, my. You think that he'd really give her a job there, and if he did, do you think she'd accept it? No way. Sam's too stubborn and way too proud to do that. Besides, she took that bakery from a place that was marginal to one of the top spots in town. You think she'd give all that up willingly?"

I pondered that for a moment. "No, I guess not. She was always headstrong and a fighter, even when I knew her back in school."

"Anyway, Sherman was always trying to push her buttons. In response, I've overheard her call him some things that I can't repeat in a church, or on the street, either. Sherman tried to get her arrested once, but Chief Jennings wouldn't do it."

That was an interesting tidbit I hadn't found out before. "Oh? What for?"

"Something about trespassing at the resort construction site. They've had problems with theft and vandalism up there. Sherman claimed he had video evidence of Sam and Dean snooping around. From what I got from the grapevine, the video wasn't clear enough to fully make them out, so Jennings did nothing but give them a stern warning."

A trip to the resort was another thing I added to my mental list of things to discuss further with Sam.

"Why do you think she didn't do it?"

"She cried over a bird once. I was at the bakery picking up a birthday cake and a robin flew into her front window and knocked itself out. Sam ran out there to see what she could do about it, and she picked that little bird up and held it until it revived and flew away. I can't imagine someone who would be so protective of a bird would take the life of anything, including a rude human."

I wasn't so sure about that. It made me daydream about the menagerie back on the bus. I've met plenty of horrible people that I'd trade in for a friendly skunk. "If Sam didn't do it, who do you suspect did? Someone stabbed Sherman. He didn't stab himself."

"I really shouldn't say." Lisa looked at the door to see if anyone might come in at that moment. I knew from experience that any time anyone said they shouldn't say, that meant they couldn't wait to spill the proverbial beans. "Dean has a terrible temper, and he's protective of Sam. They're dating. Everyone in town talks about that."

"Sam told me they weren't."

Lisa looked confused. "I don't know why she'd say that. Dean is at the diner almost every day and talks about her all the time."

Someone was lying, but I couldn't determine who. "Anyone else besides Dean? I heard Sherman wasn't much liked by many people in town."

Lisa's nose twitched. "Well, that's true. But I don't think there's anyone here who'd actually kill him. I say you don't have to look any further than Dean Williams, and that's exactly what I'm going to tell the chief first chance I get."

Lisa turned, yanked the door open, and stomped off. I washed my hands again and left the room.

CHAPTER SEVEN

I headed back to the gymnasium and stepped only a yard beyond the door when I literally bumped into Rob.

"Excuse me," he said. Rob pivoted around to determine who had run into his back, and his face displayed both delight and anguish to realize it was me. "I'm so sorry. I didn't see you."

"No, no. That's all my fault. I didn't watch where I was going. You got a second for me?" I asked.

I can't imagine where Rob's mind skipped to, but I pictured it went straight to me, inviting him back to my bus. That assumption I'd based solely on how intently he was looking to determine if his better half was watching us at the moment.

"Of course, I do," he said.

"Come with me then." I hooked my elbow into his and led him toward the stage. As we approached, I noticed Bozeman had finished packing the gear, which stood in a neat pile nearby. We couldn't leave until the cops cleared us, so Bozeman had settled into a chair with his feet up on another. He had his hat drawn low over his eyes, and a Louis L'Amour paperback in his lap. A quick glance would make you assume the book held his interest, but I guessed he was napping. He had been reading that same book for about four years, and he kept it stuffed in the pocket of his guitar case to be used more like a prop than a read. He figured people would be less likely to bother someone who was reading, and more often than not, he was right.

I led Rob onto the stage and over to the piano, where I grabbed my photo and handed it to him.

He looked at it, then looked back at me. "I like the blue hair better."

I glanced at the photo. Although I wore a hat, you still saw my long, raven black hair. I agreed. It wasn't a suitable color for me, and I never returned to it.

"Me too. I'm sorry we never got to play *Loving You, Leaving You*. I gather you were looking forward to it."

"Indeed. I'm sorry I didn't get to hear it in person."

"Hey, I got an idea. Wait here." I walked to the gear pile and returned with my guitar case. I extracted my acoustic from the case, sat on the piano bench, and played it for Rob. Even without Bozeman's accompaniment, it sounded good. The music end of it was pretty easy, just a simple, three chord progression that a billion other country songs had. But the magic of this tune I wrapped around the story it told, the story of loving someone so much you had to leave them. When I finished the song, I put the guitar away, closed up the case, and turned back to Rob. He had a tear in his eye.

"That was beautiful. That'll always be my favorite song, and I thank you for playing it for me."

I gave him an embarrassed smile and thanked him.

"Now tell me, what did you think of tonight's excitement?" I asked.

"I don't know. It all happened so fast. Sam and Sherman got into it. Then the next thing I know, Sherman took a swing at her."

"I caught that. You stepped in and saved her." I said.

"I had to. Wasn't right trying to hit a woman, no matter what she said to him."

"What did she say?"

"They argued about the bakery, and he said he had what he needed to take it from her. She called him a…"

Rob trailed off, searching for a word that he would substitute for what Sam actually said because he didn't want to repeat to me verbatim what he overheard. "… slimy weasel. Then Sam left the room while I held Sherman. After a minute or two, he pushed me off, then followed her."

Slimy weasel, not a jerk. Another inconsistency I'd need to ask Sam about.

"Did he catch her?"

"I don't know. I barely made it through the door when Lisa grabbed my arm and told me to stay out of it. She took me into the kitchen, so I can't tell you what happened after that. I didn't see Sherman again until I caught the scream and ran to the pantry."

"Who was there?" I asked.

"Shanna was the one who yelled. And I found Sam there, standing over the body. It was awful. I never want to go through anything like that again."

"Do you think Sam did it?"

"Well, she was the one closest to him, and she had his blood on her shirt, so I expect so."

"You don't consider anyone else might have done it? I understand no one around town really liked Sherman."

Rob scoffed. "Not well liked is an understatement. Everyone I know hated him. He's a cancer in this town. He even tried to start some trouble with me and Lisa down at the diner."

"Oh really? Like what?" For good measure, I batted my eyelashes at him. He didn't fall for it.

"I'm not usually for violence, but if Sam killed him, Mayor Mary should give her the key to the city." Rob held up the photo. "Thanks again for this. I'm going to frame it and hang it in the diner. I'm going to go show it to Lisa."

Rob rushed away from me like he needed to catch a train

and left me sitting there wondering what to do next. I sat for a while and watched the crowd. Besides the committee, only two dozen people waited to be cleared to leave. The clock was ticking. I had perhaps twenty minutes to finish my inquiries before the long arm of the law reached in. I sighed, stood, and planned to introduce myself to the mayor.

Mayor Mary was sitting alone. Like Shanna, she seemed busy reading something on her phone. I hoped rather than social media; the mayor was using the downtime to get through some important town business. She spotted me coming and put her phone face down on the table.

"The famous Codi Cassidy. Thanks for coming to our small town and blessing us with your music. Mary Sweets. Nice to meet you."

The mayor stuck out her hand, and I shook it.

"It was my pleasure, ma'am. I'm just sorry I didn't get to give y'all the full concert I intended."

"Well, perhaps you can come back and play during our town harvest festival in October." She seemed all business, and although she presented a warm exterior, I detected a chill just beneath her surface.

"Sure thing. Have Sam pass me along the details, and I'll check if the dates work out."

"Sam? Sam Henry?"

"Yes, she's the one who booked me for this gig. We're friends. We go way back."

"Oh, well then." She said only three simple words, but the way the mayor said them caused the temperature in the immediate area to drop by twenty degrees.

"What do you think happened here tonight? It's horrible, isn't it?" I asked.

The mayor slipped into an unannounced staring contest with me. Although it tempted me to compete, I purposely blinked several times in succession.

"Why do you care?" The mayor slid back in her seat,

checked her phone, and returned it to the table.

"Like I said, Sam's a friend, and I don't think she could have done what she's being accused of."

"I don't believe Chief Jennings has accused anyone yet. So far as I can tell, his team is still taking the initial statements of the people in attendance. Tell me, Ms. Cassidy, are you a detective?"

Her tone hardened, and I sensed a dressing down coming on. "No, ma'am."

"Perhaps you're an undercover agent with the F.B.I.? Or maybe a captain with the state police?"

I shook my head no.

"Is your napping partner over there secretly Columbo in a cowboy hat?"

I glanced over at Bozeman. He still had his feet up on a chair, but the book had fallen to the floor.

"No," I said.

"Maybe you should let the police do the police business, and if we need someone to write a ballad about it, we'll call you. Sound good?"

I recognized a dismissal when I got one, so I nodded and stepped away. Around the room I looked for Sam, saw she hadn't returned, so I wanted to share with Bozeman everything I learned and ask if he had any input. My plan traveled sideways, though, when someone wrapped a hand around my shoulder. I turned. It was Pastor Tom.

"You'll have to forgive Mayor Mary. She's under a bit of stress right now. It's not every day a benefactor of this town gets murdered in cold blood."

I wasn't sure I caught that right. "Benefactor? I found out he was trying to buy up every property he could to expand his business empire."

"Oh, no, no. It wasn't like that at all. Everything Sherman Stier did was to improve the community. Why, he had plans to update the library and city hall. Last year, the fire department moved into a larger station because of his generosity. Did you know he had plans to build an art museum dedicated to New Mexico artists? And he planned on hosting an artist's retreat yearly at the resort."

"He did, huh? Are you saying all the rumors I've been hearing about him are all wrong?"

The pastor looked in my eyes briefly, then picked a spot on my shoulder to stare at. I wondered if that was my angel's side or my devil's side.

He swallowed. "Well, you understand the human condition. No one is all good or all bad. People are by nature complicated, you understand."

Sure, I understood he didn't want to answer the question. "Yes, I get it. We're all flawed. But are you saying that everyone he threatened to ruin just misunderstood his philanthropy?"

"Did I mention the art museum? And the new fire department?"

"Yes, you did, Pastor Tom, but interestingly enough, everything you mentioned would come back and benefit him more than the town itself."

"No, you still don't understand. It's not like that at all."

"Why would someone want to stab him?" It was time to go for the blunt question. I didn't want a roundabout discussion. I never much cared for them.

"I have no clue. And I'm confident the chief will find the person responsible, and that person will go to jail, and may God have mercy on their soul after that. This is a place of God, not a place for violence. I'm sorry it had to happen here in this house of worship. What will happen to the congregation? How can people worship here without whispering about what occurred in that room? Who will clean up this mess?"

"One more question, Pastor Tom. How much money did he pledge to the church?"

Pastor Tom looked me in the eye without answering, so I supplied some options. "Ten thousand? Fifty thousand? A hundred thousand? More?"

At the word more, the good pastor's facial expressions told me all I needed.

"Strange that such an ungodly man would donate so much money to this church. What was it for? To clear his conscience? To tithe his way into heaven? Or perhaps there was something else going on. Was there, Pastor?"

His countenance changed, and I guessed there was, although I didn't know what. Yet another question I could add to my ever-expanding list of questions without answers.

"Have a good evening, Miss Cassidy. I will pray for you tonight."

Pastor Tom hastily moved away to the far side of the room. I couldn't tell what was going on with him, but I always hated to be called 'miss'. Did I look like a 'miss'? Come to think of it, with my small stature and my blue hair, I probably did, but that was well beside the point.

I was still stewing when I felt a tap on my shoulder. Once I spun around, I recognized the man in the uniform. I guess it was my turn with Chief Jennings.

"Chief Jennings, I presume?"

"Codi Cassidy, right? I apologize for being gruff before, but I couldn't have a suspect speaking to anyone. You mind answering a few questions?"

"Of course."

"Is Codi Cassidy your real name or a stage name?"

"Real name. Codi Lynn Cassidy. That's Codi ending with an I, not a Y."

"And your address and phone number."

I gave him a business card with the address of my post office box in Utah, along with my cell phone number and email address. He copied everything from the card down into a notebook, then put the business card in his shirt pocket.

"You don't have a physical address?"

I smiled. "My physical address is anywhere we park that bus out back. The post office box is a mail forwarding service. I have it to get the important stuff, like bills and my magazines. If you need to contact me, the best way is through text or email."

"Get a ton of fan mail, do you?" The question seemed innocent enough, but there was an underlying snarky tone to it.

I threw him a sweet smile. "I get a fair amount."

The glance he threw at me told me he didn't believe it. But it was true. I usually received ten or twelve fan letters a month, and that number typically tripled around my birthday.

"In your own words, can you tell me what happened here tonight? Anything you may have seen or heard?"

I sunk into the nearest chair to get comfortable. Chief Jennings stayed standing in his power position. I wondered if he meant what I saw and heard as an eyewitness, or saw and heard with all the snooping around I'd been doing over the past hour. I went with the former.

"There's not much I can tell you, chief. I spent most of my night on or near the stage. The only exception was when we had our meal break."

"Who's we?"

I pointed in Bozeman's direction. "Me and my partner, Bozeman James."

The chief raised an eyebrow. "Is that his real name?"

"I think his birth name is Jesse, but I've only ever known him as Bozeman."

"What can you tell me about the altercation?"

"I didn't witness any of that. I didn't know there was one until you stopped the show."

The chief looked up at me. "I don't mean the murder. I mean, the fight that happened right before."

"Like I said, Chief Jennings, I caught little of it since I was on stage performing my set. I witnessed Sherman push Sam, and when Sherman took a swing at her, a couple of guys stepped in and stopped him. Then, so far as I guessed, it was over. That's all I can really tell you."

The chief continued his notes, then closed his book. "How

well do you know Samantha Henry? Rumor has it you're the best of friends."

That information didn't take long to get back to him.

"I wouldn't say that we're the best of friends. We were classmates back in high school, but I hadn't seen or heard from her after graduation until a couple of months ago."

"Why did she contact you?"

For the head of the police department, the guy seemed to be a dim bulb, and it shouldn't take remedial math to put this two and two together. "Well, she was in charge of the entertainment, and I'm an entertainer, so…" I held my arms out, hoping he'd make the connection all on his own.

"And you don't find it suspicious that she'd hire you out of the blue?"

"No. Not really. I get lots of contacts from people I've known in my past. Especially when they learn I'm coming back through town and they're looking for free tickets to the rodeo or something. Occasionally old friends like Sam will hire us to play gigs. Usually private parties or events like this one."

"People have seen you with her frequently over the last couple of days."

I didn't understand what he wanted to imply, but I didn't plan to fall for it. I usually had a long rope, but I was getting to the end. "Yes. We, meaning Bozeman and I, got to town around four-thirty yesterday afternoon. I ran into her when I was walking around town, and we talked for a bit. Then we ate dinner at the diner, and this morning I spent some time with her at the bakery. I'm not sure what it is you're digging for, but you will not find it. We're old friends, and if you think it's suspicious that old friends would want to reconnect after a long time, then I feel sorry for you."

"Did Sam ever say she wanted to kill Sherman Stier or anything like that?"

"No. Of course not. Why are you so focused on Sam? There were a couple hundred people here tonight, and any of them could have done it."

"And every single person here tonight is getting questioned, but the way it looks to us is that the evidence points right at your friend. She had the motive. She had the opportunity. She had his blood on her, she found the body, she had a vendetta, and most importantly, the knife recovered at the scene belonged to her."

"How could you possibly figure that out that already?" I sounded way too defensive, and I suspected I had to tone down my emotion. I had to remain calm and rational, so I took a cleansing breath. "Surely you couldn't have figured that out this quick, even if you were a top-notch detective."

Chief Jennings grinned. It didn't suit him. "It didn't take a detective. She engraved her name on the handle. So, if it walks like a duck..."

He had me there. It didn't look good for Sam. "Yeah, yeah. I got it. It's a duck."

"Of course, like I said, we're questioning everyone here. Everyone is a suspect as far as the law is concerned until we have definitive evidence that points to someone. Sam will get a fair shake from me."

I didn't know if I believed him, but I thanked him anyway, and he left me and headed over to Bozeman. Bozeman had woken from his nap, and their exchange didn't take long. Once Bozeman was alone again, I approached him.

"What did he say?" I asked.

Bozeman put his hat on the table and ran his fingers through his hair. "Probably the same things he said to you. We're free to go tonight, but we need to stick around town for a couple of days."

"He didn't mention that part to me."

"He probably assumed you would stick around, anyway. Let's get the bus loaded."

I hoped to talk to Sam again, but I didn't see her. A deputy had taped off an area around the back door, and cleanup had begun in the rest of the room. Lisa and Rob were supervising the removal of the remaining dinner service. Hanson was still collecting centerpieces, and Dean was helping Reba to her feet. I hadn't seen Shanna since I talked to her, so I assumed she was back in the kitchen. The mayor had disappeared, as had Pastor Tom.

Bozeman was in a hurry to get the bus loaded, so he rushed me along to get the job done. Once we loaded up, I got out of my gig clothes and slipped into my comfy jeans and tennis shoes. I added a jean jacket and a baseball cap to my ensemble and found Bozeman, who was already behind the wheel.

"Hey, I'm going to walk back to the lot, okay? I really need the fresh air."

Bozeman gave me the look. "Are you sure it's safe?"

"No. But I'm going to do it, anyway."

Bozeman sighed. "At least take Betty with you."

I reached around to my back and felt for Betty, already tucked into the holster, and hidden by my jacket. Betty was only a .22, and I always loaded her with nonlethal rounds. I made sure the probability was as low as possible that I'd actually kill someone, but it was all about having a deterrent available. "Already done."

Bozeman nodded. "Good. Don't dawdle. If you're not back at the bus in thirty minutes, I'm coming out looking for you."

"Deal." I stepped off the bus, helped guide Bozeman out of the parking lot, then headed out on foot.

Truth be told, I enjoyed wandering around at night, even if it was a little more dangerous. There was something about being out in the evening air that revived my spirit, and I often got song or poetry ideas while meandering around. Bozeman thought it was silly and dangerous for me to venture out like I do, but I disagree with him about it every time. Bozeman's the type who sees danger around every corner, and I'm nowhere near that paranoid, even if they are really out to get me.

I came to a corner, turned it, and took a few steps. As I walked past the church's main door, I realized I had ventured off in the wrong direction, so I did a one-hundred-eighty-degree turn and headed the other way. If it was one thing I hated, it was being directionally challenged. It was okay, though, because I always got to where I wanted to go, even if it took me a little extra mileage to get there.

I walked up the quiet road toward Main Street and noticed how dead it was. I had been to towns before where everything seemed to shut down at sunset, and this seemed to be one of those towns. Up ahead, a car passed by occasionally, but it was a rare sight. I passed a few houses with the curtains drawn, and behind them I could see flickering lights, so I knew it was television time in western America.

Past the houses, I came across a business. Was it one block of businesses before I got to Main Street, or two? I couldn't remember. I really needed to pay closer attention to my environment, which should be easy since I never have to drive, so I made a mental note to do just that. Another few steps and I passed an alley and then found myself in front of an electronics sales and repair shop. In the front window stood a variety of the old-time radios that people used to sit in front of before the TV came along. There was a single lamp burning inside the shop. By that light, I saw there were console televisions, giant old stereos, and even a couple of computers that must have dated back to the eighties. I wasn't sure how much of the shop was for sales and repairs versus how much of the shop was a museum of lost technologies.

Down toward Main Street I continued, my heels clicking on the concrete. I stopped again, glanced down at the soft-soled shoes I was wearing. No clicks. The hair on the back of my neck rose as I realized I was being followed. I continued walking down to the next storefront, then stopped and quickly pivoted. I didn't see anyone behind me.

Come on, Codi, get it together. No reason to get the jitters.

I started walking again and increased my pace until I was almost jogging. The clicking started again. Finally, I saw the traffic lights of Main Street half a block down. I hurried along, then as soon as I turned the corner, I dipped into the first inset entryway and extracted Betty from the holster and tucked her in my jacket pocket.

I waited and I counted to ten, then inched my head out to see if anyone was on the sidewalk. The coast was clear, so I stepped from the doorway, and crept back to the corner and glanced around the building. Nothing. I didn't realize I'd been holding my breath until I exhaled. I looked down Main Street and saw a group of teenagers milling around in front of a sandwich shop, so I jaywalked across the street and headed in their direction. As I got closer to them, I slowed down my stride and took a couple of furtive glances behind me. I still didn't see anyone.

Rather than continue on alone, I slipped into the shop.

"I'm sorry, we're closing up," the man behind the counter said.

"Look. I think there's someone following me. Can I wait in here for just a few minutes? I won't get in your way."

The man stepped around the counter, walked out the door, and came back in a minute later. "There's no one out there. Street's empty."

I didn't move. "Please. Just give me a couple of minutes."

The man stepped back to the counter and picked up where he left off with his cleaning. "I haven't seen you around here before."

"No. I'm from out of town. I was out for a walk and wasn't paying attention to where I was going, so I ended up on some side street."

"Where are you staying?"

Sometimes I believe that little white lies are much better options than telling the truth, so I lied. "The Quincey Inn. On Main Street. Where is that from here?"

The man pointed to the right. "Down that way, about six or seven blocks. You need me to walk you over there?"

I went to the door and looked outside. Not a soul in sight. "No. I think I'm okay now. It was probably nothing but my active imagination. It's always getting me into trouble. Thank you, though."

Before the man could respond, I left the shop and trotted up Main Street. I slowed four blocks later when the bakery came into view. Bozeman was at the corner waiting for me. He must have seen me coming up the street because he wore a look of concern on his face.

"Pleasant walk?"

I bent over, put my hands on my knees, and breathed deep a few times. "Could have been better."

CHAPTER EIGHT

At six the next morning, I was up, out of bed, and ready to go. I fed Gibson and filled a food bowl full of vegetables for Merle and Dolly. Since Sunday was treat day, I pulled some worms from the fridge for Merle, and opened a can of salmon for Dolly. There was no way to forget about Willie and Waylon, so I cut up half an apple for Willie, and half a banana for Waylon. I ate the other half of each fruit for my breakfast. Quiet not to wake Bozeman, I slipped out of the bus with the various food bowls and distributed them where they needed to go. Since daybreak was fast approaching, Merle and Dolly were still wide awake when I dropped off their dishes. Waylon and Willie were still in their little nest, dreaming about whatever chipmunks dream about, so I left the food outside.

In the breaking dawn, I stepped over to the bakery's back door. The door wouldn't budge, so I went around to the front. I saw the sign and realized I made a mistake. It was Sunday, and the bakery was closed for the day.

"Hey, you." The voice descended from above, and it startled me and made me jump back from the door. I took another step closer to the street and looked up. Sam was sitting on a small balcony drinking a cup of coffee. "Directly to your left is a door. It's unlocked. Come on up."

I found the door and took the stairs to the second floor, and Sam had the door to her home open before I hit the top step.

"Nice place." I looked around at the small, tidy space.

"It came with the bakery. It makes for a short commute in the morning. Would you like some coffee?"

"I'm more of a tea person."

"This is your lucky day. Follow me."

I tailed Sam into the kitchen. It was small, but functional. Sam filled a kettle with water and placed it on the stove to boil, then reached into a cabinet and found a mug. "Hey, I hope a tea bag is okay. I don't have any loose tea."

I laughed. "Steeping a bag is the only way I know how to make it."

Sam handed me a box of assorted fruit-based teas, and I selected a cherry one, opened the package, and dropped the bag in the mug. We waited in silence for the kettle to whistle, and when it did, Sam filled the mug. "Honey? Sugar?"

"Honey, please. That would be great."

Sam handed me a plastic bear of honey and I stirred in a dollop while Sam topped off her coffee. We took our beverages into the living room. Sam sat on the couch and threw a blanket over her bare legs. I sat in the only other chair in the room. I noticed she was still wearing my T-shirt.

"Rough night." I tried to take a sip, but the tea was too hot yet, so I held the mug between my hands to warm them.

"One of the roughest I've ever had," Sam said.

"What happened to you? I wanted to talk to you more, but you disappeared."

"Not by choice. When the chief saw me talking to you, he blew a gasket and had a deputy take me into the station. I had to wait there until the chief got back from questioning everyone else. I've only been home for a few hours. It seems I'm his prime suspect, and he's going to arrest me the second they process the evidence. Lucky for him, it all points back to me."

I stirred my tea and took a sip. "How do you know that?" I asked.

"Because that's a direct quote. So much for justice being blind, right?"

"Sam, look at me." Sam raised her eyes and looked directly into mine. "Did you do it? Did you kill Sherman Stier?"

Her gaze never wavered. "No, I didn't."

I could detect nothing in her voice or her body language to tell me she was lying.

"I talked to quite a few people last night. About half seem convinced you did," I said. I had a few sips of tea.

Sam took a drink of coffee, but then didn't respond.

"Sam, how did your knife get there?"

She drained the mug and set it on the table beside her. "I don't know. I took a few items to the church. Like a couple of pie cutters and three or four knives, but that knife was my favorite, so I wouldn't have taken it for fear of it getting stolen or misplaced."

"Why take anything? You told me the church had all the equipment you needed in the pantry."

"Yeah, but people donated most of the things they have and nothing is in the best of condition. It's not unusual for us to bring our own things in for the evening. Ask the McMurtrys. They do the same thing."

"What about Dean? Lots of people I talked to seemed to imply you two are dating, but you said otherwise."

"Because we're not. Like I said, we went out two or three times, and he was the sweetest guy ever. Then I made the mistake of sleeping with him, and he became downright possessive after that. That's when I broke things off. I can't be in that kind of relationship again."

I believed her. As far as I was concerned, she was three for three on the truth meter. Time for the big one. "Okay. What really went down with Sherman?"

Sam hesitated while she folded her blanket over to cover her bare calf. "He pinched me on the butt. Without even thinking, I spun around and grabbed him by his jangly parts and told him to never do that again or I'd castrate him. That's when he pushed me. So, then I made a wisecrack about his lack of manhood, and that's when he tried to take a swing at me. I guess I got him where it hurt him the most, huh?"

Sam chuckled at the memory. I smiled along with her. "Well, if you didn't kill him, we need to find out who did. Is the diner open on Sundays?"

Sam looked at a clock on the wall. It was one of those hanging cat ones where the tail and eyes moved. I thought those only existed in the movies. "It opens in fifteen minutes."

I got up and collected the mugs. "Then let's go get some pancakes. You go get dressed and I'll clean this stuff up."

By seven-thirty, we walked into the diner and grabbed the last table. It took me about three seconds of glancing at the menu to decide on the blueberry pancakes with a side of bacon. Sam, who said she didn't have an appetite, ordered raisin toast and coffee.

"The way I've worked it out, it's got to be someone on the committee," I said as I unfolded and refolded my napkin. "Although I talked to them last night, I'd like to talk to everyone again today to see if anyone saw or heard anything, or if anyone seems like a viable suspect."

"Do you really believe anyone on the committee can kill someone?"

"Would you prefer you remain the prime person of focus?" I asked.

"Um, no. After a second thought, perhaps someone on the committee did do it."

I unfolded and refolded my napkin again. One glance at Sam told me I was getting on Sam's nerves, so I put my napkin on my lap and started sorting the packets of sugar substitute by color instead. I hated waiting for meals to be served. I never knew what to do with my hands.

The server brought the food at last. Sam's raisin toast looked homemade, and my pancakes were larger than my head. After I covered them with butter, I added a portion of maple syrup. I forked off a corner and took a bite. I moaned in pleasure.

"My goodness gracious, that's delicious. Those blueberries just pop with flavor. Are they the same ones you use in your muffins?"

Sam brushed a toast crumb from her shirt. "Yes. We have the same supplier. Normally you can't grow blueberries in New Mexico, but there's a farmer in the next county over who specializes in them. He has whole greenhouses dedicated to fruits and vegetables that don't come from this area."

"How's the toast?" I asked.

Sam smiled. "It's perfect. I made the bread yesterday. What's the matter?"

"Nothing, it's just…" I took another bite and ran through the mental notes in my head while I chewed. "Yesterday, someone mentioned something about Stier destroying the diner's supply chain. I can't remember who I talked to, though."

"Is that relevant?"

I smiled. "It is if it gives someone else a motive."

I ate about half of the pancakes, and two out of three slices of bacon. Sam ate the remaining slice for me. Off in the distance, I saw Lisa, so I got her attention and waved her over.

"Good morning. Everything okay with your meal?" Lisa asked when she got to us.

"It was perfect," I answered. "Probably the best pancakes I've ever had. Listen, can I ask you a couple of questions? About last night?"

Lisa looked around the diner. "I really shouldn't. We're really busy this morning."

I gave her the puppy dog eyes. "Please? I'll only take a few minutes of your time, then I won't bother you again until I stalk you later for the pancake recipe."

Lisa scanned the area again. Everything looked to be running smoothly. "Okay, but I can only spare a couple of minutes." Lisa took the seat between Sam and me, and I asked her about what she saw or heard the previous evening. She added no further information from the night before, and her story didn't change.

I redirected the questions. "Is the diner going to be okay?"

A look of confusion crossed Lisa's face like a passing cloud. "Why wouldn't it be?"

"A little birdie told me that when they build the new resort, you're going to lose all your food suppliers and you'll need to close your doors. Now that Stier is gone, I imagine the diner is safe."

Lisa gave me the sternest look I've ever seen and seemed poised to give me the largest denial in history. The storm passed at once. Her face softened, and she threw me a smile as sweet as the pancake syrup at our table.

"You've been talking to Reba, haven't you? You got that nugget from her? She often mishears things, and then likes to repeat, incorrectly, I might add, the things she misheard. Yes, we have a lot of local suppliers, and we'd have to compete with any new restaurant for their business. Including Sam here. You know we get those blueberries from the same place?"

"Yes, she told me."

"Well then. However, even if a supplier can't fill an order, we have contingencies plans in place. Come with me."

Lisa took off from her chair, and I followed as close behind her as I could. We moved from the dining room through the swinging door in the kitchen. Behind the flattop was Rob, and around him were two other cooks, trying to keep up with the flurry of incoming orders. Lisa stopped in front of a large door, pulled it open, and gestured for me to join her in the walk-in freezer. The door slammed shut behind us, and the immediate chill hit me like a whack in the head from a tennis racket.

Lisa scraped the frost off a cardboard box. "Here, take a gander at that."

I read the box. Frozen beef. The box next to it held chicken breasts, the next contained pork. Lisa turned around and pushed the door open, and I followed, happy to leave the cold. She led me into another room where I saw large cans of fruits and vegetables. Along with them sat bags of various grains and even a couple of industrial sized boxes of instant potatoes.

From the pantry, Lisa led me to the small office and took a seat behind the desk. There was no other chair, so she pointed to the two-drawer file cabinet, and I sat on that.

"We try to be as farm-to-table as we can be, but the fact is that there are always supply chain issues and we have contingencies to deal with them. All that frozen meat you saw, all the canned goods? They all come from a distributor in Arizona. Here, look."

Lisa spun in her seat and grabbed a clipboard that was hanging on the wall. She flipped over a couple of pages and passed it to me. It was an invoice, one for ground beef, from a place in Tucson.

"If you opened that bottom drawer below you, you'd find lots of other paperwork showing the same." I had no reason to believe otherwise, so I didn't budge.

"We even have a backup plan if Sam doesn't come through with the baked goods we use. None of the frozen or canned food comes out as well as we'd normally serve, but we always tell our customers when there's a change. Believe me, in this part of the world, everyone is more than familiar with food, fuel, weather, or water disruptions."

I handed the clipboard back, and she returned it to its hook on the wall. "So, then the resort wouldn't have affected your business at all."

Lisa shook her head. "If it did anything, it may have made things crazier around here. I would imagine that there are some folks who would come into town for more of a home cooked meal rather than eat whatever option they had at the new resort."

I nodded. "You're probably right. I'm sorry I took up your time. No hard feelings?"

Lisa approached and took me into a hug. "Of course not. I know what you're doing and are looking out for Sam, and I appreciate that. Rob and I both love her to death, and to be honest, we need her here. She's just as much a part of this restaurant's success as we are."

She let me go and escorted me back to the dining room where I retook my seat.

"Well?" Sam asked.

"So far as I can tell, it checks out. I don't think they had the motive to kill Stier. They have a distributor they use if they can't source food from around here."

Sam shrugged.

"But you knew that already," I continued.

Sam nodded.

"Because you do the same thing."

Sam smiled. "Yes, I do. We use some of the same people, actually. I source mostly dry ingredients from their people. Flour, sugar, baking soda, that kind of stuff. Oh, and fruit when I can't get it fresh. My primary concern is typically eggs, but I also use a fair amount of dairy, like butter, milk, and cream. All depends on what I'm making."

"Wouldn't the resort cut into your dairy and egg sources?"

"Not really. I work with mostly smaller farmers, ones that wouldn't be able to handle that large a contract, anyway. And even if the resort somehow cut into the business, I'm not worried. It wouldn't be the first time I'd have to drive over to Tucson or El Paso for supplies. Oh, and honey. I have a local supplier for honey, but I could easily get by with store-bought stuff."

"What about chocolate?"

"Again, I wouldn't be affected. I'm a little particular about the chocolate I use, but I've teamed up with a bakery in Las Cruces that uses the same stuff I do. They're bigger than I am, so we go in on an order together and it gets shipped to them, then about once a month I head over there and pick up what I ordered."

"So, what you're saying is?"

"I agree with you, Codi. Rob and Lisa didn't do it. They didn't need to. They'll be fine with or without the resort. So now what?"

"Let's go over and see Reba. I'd be interested in seeing what she had to say."

Sam checked her watch. "It's after eight. We could wander that way and see if she's up."

"Why wouldn't she be? She owns a bed-and-breakfast, and she told me she's fully booked, so wouldn't she have to give her patrons breakfast?"

Sam stood, and I followed her out of the restaurant. "Breakfast is a loose term over there. She mostly offers cereals, packaged oatmeal, pastries wrapped in plastic wrap, that kind of thing."

I never noticed how fast Sam walked. I almost had to do double time to keep up with her. "That must thrill the vacationers."

"She makes up for it in the afternoon with a wine and cheese experience. Come on, we can walk over. It's only about eight blocks from here. You good with that?"

"Sure. Just slow down, okay?"

Sam dropped her speed in half, and I could resume a normal stride. I didn't mind the walk, and it was a beautiful morning. If I had to guess, the temperature was in the lower sixties, and there was a light breeze coming in from the south. We continued on in silence, and I wondered what must be going through Sam's mind. The last few hours must have been nothing but stress for her.

I was walking along, looking at a marvelous flower garden across the street when I slammed directly into Sam's back when she halted. I took a step backward, caught my heel on the sidewalk, and plopped to my rear.

"Are you okay? Anything hurt?" Sam asked as she offered me a hand up.

"Only my pride. Sorry about that. I wasn't paying attention."

Sam shrugged and pointed at a lovely, well kept Victorian home in front of us. "We're here, and I don't think we'll have to roust Reba from bed."

I looked to the house and noticed the old woman sitting in a rocking chair on the large front porch. She appeared to be napping. I approached her, trying to make as much noise as possible along the way.

"Ms. Reba? Hello?" I reached out for the chair's arm and gave it a gentle rock.

Reba's eyes sprung open like she got hit with a dose of adrenaline. She looked up at me. "I served the breakfast in the dining room off the kitchen."

"I'm not here for breakfast. Remember me from last night?" I took off my baseball cap and let my hair fall free. "You asked about my blue hair. Remember?"

She didn't seem to at first, but then she snapped to. "Of course, I remember. I'm not senile, you know!"

"Oh, I'm sorry. I meant no disrespect." I put my hat back on and crouched in front of her. "Can I ask you a few more questions about last night?"

Reba didn't seem sure, but she nodded anyway. I asked her the same things I had the night before, and she responded with more or less the same answers, although this time she left out Stevie's tax trouble. She was hazy on anything too detailed, and I chalked that up to the wine. This conversation led down to another dead end.

"You have a lovely home. Have you always lived here?"

She motioned for me to sit in the rocking chair next to hers, and for the benefit of my aching knees, I did.

"I was born in this house, as was my mother. This was one

of the first houses ever built in this city. It was the mayor's house back in the day."

"Tell me more about it."

"Well, I used to live on the top floor, but once I got a little older, I moved to the ground floor. I converted a small office and sitting room into a little two room living quarters for myself. There are four bedrooms on the second floor, and a suite and another bedroom on the third. Has all the original woodwork, and the fireplaces are original as well. It's the best place to stay in town."

Sam tittered.

"What's so funny?" I asked.

"Since the motel closed last summer, it's the only place to stay besides the Quincey Inn."

Reba took offense and shook her frail fist in Sam's direction. "You build a hundred hotels, and this place would still be the best."

"I'd love to check it out. I love old houses," I said.

Reba shifted in her chair and pointed to the door. "Go on in. I have guests in every room at the moment, so don't go past the first floor, but you're welcome to look around."

I smiled, told them I'd be right back, and stepped into the house. The room I entered appeared to be the new sitting room, and it was marvelous. There were four large chairs at different spots around the room, and a table in the center. On the table was a chess game already in progress. From what I could tell, black was going to win in about four moves. On one wall was a fireplace, and where there weren't doorways or windows, there were floor to ceiling bookcases, each of them stuffed full of books. I walked through the room and scanned the shelves at random. There appeared to be a variety of things to read, from a leather-bound edition of Shakespeare's works to old western paperbacks. There were a few romance novels mixed in, along with a few contemporary thriller writers that I recognized. It was a nice home library where anyone could come in and find something to read.

There was a door to the left of the entryway, and I turned the knob and pushed it open. It appeared to be Reba's bedroom. She hadn't made the bed, and there were clothes piled on a chair. I closed the door behind me and continued down the hallway. The next room I encountered was a dining room with an enormous table that sat twelve easily. The furniture looked to be period pieces in great shape. There was a couple at the table eating breakfast, so I said hello and continued on to the kitchen.

Unlike the dining room, the kitchen was more contemporary in style. The stove, dishwasher, and refrigerator looked fairly new. I confirmed my suspicions when I saw the energy efficiency sticker on the fridge's side where one would hang magnets. Above and below, the cabinets were beautiful and looked recently repainted, and I looked at the floor. The hardwood gleamed compared to what I'd seen in the other rooms. Complete with the tour, I returned to the porch.

"It really is lovely. I like the kitchen. Was it redone recently?" I asked.

Reba nodded. "There was a sewer problem that damaged the lines underneath the kitchen. Had to tear the whole thing apart to fix it."

"That must have been horrible for you."

"You bet it was. The topper was the city wanted me to pay for it all, even though it was their problem. Can you imagine that?"

"How did that work out?"

"Well, deary, I contacted my insurance company who sent an insurance adjuster lady over, and she looked over the whole mess, and do you know what she said?"

How could I? "No. What did she say?"

"She said the city was liable and there was no way the insurance was going to pay. Then she got on the phone to some bigwig city lawyer, and a week later, some contractors were over here giving me options for new stuff. Can you dig it?"

I nodded. I dug it.

"You're sold out until fall?" I asked.

Reba nodded. "Yep. Things don't die down for me until after the fall festival. Then after that, I give the house a top to bottom deep cleaning, and I leave town for a couple of months."

"Where do you go?"

"My sister lives over in San Diego. I go there for Thanksgiving, and I'm back here after New Year's. Got to be back for Valentine's Day. That's a big seller for me too. I can really raise the rates then, and people pay 'em if you get my meaning."

I got it, so I smiled and nodded. "How would it affect you if they built the resort? Would you still do all that business?"

Reba leaned over and let out a puff of air. "I don't care."

The answer surprised me. "Why not?"

"Blue hair lady, I'm eighty-four years old. The only reason I run this here business is to make enough to pay the property taxes and supplement my social security. And I enjoy having the people around for company. I'd be just as happy to move closer to my sister. Weather's nicer there, anyway."

"But what about this house? Your family legacy?"

Reba cackled at me. "You're a funny one. Someday, probably soon, I'm going to die, and it won't be more than a hundred years later, and this town will be dead right along with me. Eventually this house will rot away, and we'll both be worm food. Nothing lasts forever, even though people will tell you otherwise. Now if you don't mind, I need to see to my boarders."

Reba struggled to rise, yet stood without help, then shuffled into the house and closed the large front door behind her. I guessed we were no longer welcome.

Sam started down the walkway. "Well, did she do it?"

"No, Sam, I don't think she did."

"Because she didn't care about the resort?"

"Did you see her get in the house? She could barely grip the doorknob. I think she's got a severe case of arthritis going on there. Not only did she not have a motive to kill Sherman Stier, she wouldn't have had the strength to do it."

"So now what?"

"Now, my dear Watson, we move on to the next person."

CHAPTER NINE

We took the short walk over to the flower shop and found the door locked and the closed sign in the window. It didn't surprise me as it looked like most of Main Street seemed deserted. It appeared the few businesses that opened on a Sunday wouldn't open until late morning.

I knocked on the door a few times and peered through the window. All I saw were plants, no humans. "I guess it's a strikeout. Do you know where Hanson lives?"

"On the west side of town, on the other side of the tracks," Sam said.

"Every time someone says that phrase, I wonder which side of the tracks is the good side," I said.

Sam smiled. "This is Quincey. Both sides of the tracks are fine. We consider the west side of the tracks the newer part of town because the homes over there are less than fifty years old. He moved out there when his parents moved out of town."

"Do you have a number for him? I'd really like to talk to him again, and I'd like you to be there. He wasn't exactly warm to me last night."

"Yeah, he can run hot or cold based on his mood, and if he gets into his defensive posture, he tucks his head into his shell like a turtle. It's just the way he is. I'm sure he'll come around."

"So, you have his number?"

Sam patted me on the shoulder. "Of course. I've got it in my address book at home. Speaking of home, do you mind if we call him a little later? I didn't sleep last night, and I'd really love to take a nap."

I would've preferred not to wait, but it was Sam under the spotlight, not me. If she needed a nap, I'd let her have one since I'd rather have a sharp Sam than a sleep deprived one. I looked at her and recognized she had bags under her eyes, and she looked exhausted. "Sure thing. Take all the time you need."

"I only need an hour or two. Will you be on your bus?"

"Yes. I don't plan on heading anywhere without you, so I'll wait for you there. I'm sure after a nap and a long shower, you'll feel a lot more alive."

Sam and I parted company, and I watched her disappear behind the door. I stepped around the side of the building and headed toward the bus. The lawn chairs were set up, so I assumed Bozeman had to be awake and about. As I got closer to the bus, I noticed that Waylon and Willie were out, and one or both of them had tipped over their bowl and were busy eating their snacks from the ground. They detected my approach, and both stopped, sat up, and looked in my direction. When they saw it was me, they returned to their feast. When I got to them, I bent over to pick up the bowl and Willie skittered over to me. I scratched his head and accepted the chunk of apple he held up to me.

"Aw, thanks, buddy. I had a big breakfast though, so I'm full. Why don't you take this back so it doesn't go to waste?"

Willie chirped at me, grabbed the apple from my fingers, stuffed it into his little cheeks, and ran back to Waylon.

I stepped onto the bus. Bozeman was in the kitchen making his breakfast. "Want some eggs?" he asked.

"No, thanks. I've eaten already." I didn't have the heart to tell him about the superb pancakes I had, especially since his eggs were always just on the edge of inedible. He tried, though.

I moved into my room, grabbed a book from the table, and I noticed I had left my phone there as well. I was one of those people who constantly misplaced their phone, so I often made a habit of leaving it in my room. Bozeman lectured me several times over the years about having it on me. He insisted it was for my own benefit. I could call him if I needed to, or hail a cab, or use it to get directions when I got lost, but I still hadn't gotten into the habit. I stuffed the phone into my pocket and headed back to the kitchen.

"Early morning?" Bozeman slid the eggs out of the pan and onto a plate. He grabbed a fork and sat at the table. I noticed he didn't have his coffee with him, so I poured him a mug and handed it to him. Like all cowboys, he took it black, with no sugar. I reached into a cabinet and pulled out a diet cola, my choice for my daily caffeine intake.

"Yeah. I was with Sam. We went to see the McMurtrys at the diner, and Reba."

"Find out anything useful?" Bozeman asked between bites.

I exhaled. "Yeah, none of them did it. Sam wanted a nap. We're going back out later. Want to come?"

"No thanks. I'll leave the detective work to you if you don't mind."

I smiled and left him with his eggs. I carried my book and cola outside and set them beside my lawn chair. Before I sat down, I put my head into Dolly and Merle's compartment. They were both present, accounted for, and napping. The bowls I gave them earlier were empty, so I pulled them out. Merle opened his eyes when I removed the bowl, then turned over and nodded back to sleep. Dolly never moved. They each had their own blanket, and I moved Dolly over a bit to check under hers. Dolly liked to collect stuff. I always checked her treasure haul to make sure she didn't get her paws on something that might be hazardous to either her or her roommate. She must have been scavenging during the night, because she had hidden under the blanket a penny, a bottle cap from a beer, three shiny rocks, and a stem with leaves. I confiscated everything except the rocks. Dolly liked rocks.

The penny and bottle cap I put into my pocket. I'd put the penny in the mug on my desk, and the bottle cap in the trash. The stem I was about to toss away, when I noticed there was a sticky substance on the end. I stepped into the sun and brought it closer and stared at it. It looked like a piece of thin green tape, and the edges of the leaves had a white dust on them.

"Dolly, what did you find here? And where did you get it?" There were times it tempted me to put a mini helmet on Dolly with a camera attached. I'd love to see where she traveled on her adventures, but since she didn't have one, this was just a mystery. I didn't know if the plant was poisonous or not, so I set it on the bus step as a reminder to throw it away when I tossed the bottle cap.

I took a seat, had a drink of cola, and opened the book. According to the bookmark, I was on page twenty, but when I glanced at the cover, I couldn't remember what the book was about. Was it something I started reading, or had I shoved the bookmark at a random spot to make sure I had one? I couldn't tell for sure, so I flipped back to page one and started the book from the beginning.

I shifted in my seat. Impatience was eating at me, and I couldn't concentrate. I read the same page repeatedly, and although I understood what the words on the page were, I couldn't get them to assemble in my brain to form the story they told.

I was reading through page one for the fourth time when a black SUV with dark, tinted windows pulled into the lot and came to a stop less than a foot from my seat. The engine revved for a second, and then the car shut off. I stayed where I was, and as I wondered who might be up for a Sunday morning visit,

Mayor Mary stepped out of the vehicle. She wore blue jeans, a plaid western shirt, and the same scowl on her face I remembered from the night before.

"Good morning, Mayor." I put a little lilt in my voice to sound extra-friendly. "It's got the making of a beautiful day today."

The mayor stepped in front of me and removed her sunglasses. "I would've thought you'd left town by now."

I put my book on my lap. I didn't bother with the bookmark. "No, ma'am. Chief Jennings asked us to stay around for a couple of days in case he had any further questions for us."

"I'm sure that would be an inconvenience for you, since I imagine you have another performance to get to. I can square it with the chief so you can leave today. Don't worry. I'll call him just as soon as church lets out."

She was being pushy. I can be that way too, sometimes. "Thank you, but that's unnecessary. Our next gig isn't for a few days yet, and it's only a day's drive away, so we're in no hurry to leave. Besides, I like this town. Have you had the blueberry pancakes down at the diner? Delicious."

Mayor Mary smiled through clenched teeth. "I'm sure there are more… interesting places to visit on your way."

I doubted that. "Let's cut to it, Mayor, all the way down to the proverbial brass tacks. Why the bum's rush to get us out of town?"

Mayor Mary stared at me for what felt like an hour. I could tell there was something she wanted to say. I guessed since she was a bureaucrat; she was trying to find a delicate way to say it that wouldn't reflect poorly on her. That approach always rubbed me the wrong way, and I wanted to cut her off, but I waited.

"It's not like that at all. Look, even though you're just a musician, you're also a businessperson, correct? I'm sure you can understand what kind of pressure I'm under trying to do what's best for this town, and sometimes that involves making hard decisions. Look, I get it that people around here are talking about me, and how I invited Sherman Stier and his associates into the area, but it really was for the good of the community."

Did I catch that right? That she invited them in? That was a nugget I hadn't heard from anyone. "Like a new fire station or an art museum?"

The mayor smiled. "Exactly. Everyone will benefit from those. Just like everyone will benefit from increased tourism that the resort will bring. Business will be up, the tax base will increase, and I won't have to beg the state constantly for infrastructure improvement dollars. In the end, everyone wins."

Her words made sense, but I assumed that as a politician, she filled them with only half-truths. I took them with more than a grain of salt.

"Are you from Quincey, Mayor?"

"Why yes, I am. My family has been here for generations. My great-great-grandfather worked on the railroad, and my grandfather worked in a mine near here. I left town to attend college, but I came back home to be closer to family."

"That's nice. I'm sure your folks are really proud of you becoming mayor."

Mayor Mary grinned, the most authentic smile I'd seen her produce in the short time I've known her. "Yes, very. I'm the first female mayor in Quincey history."

"Congratulations. That's quite the accomplishment." I was genuine. I was all for girl-power. "Look, I don't mean to ruffle your feathers. Sam is still upset about what happened yesterday, and I want to stay around for just a couple of days to make sure she's okay. I'm sure you'd do the same for your friends, right?"

The mayor nodded, turned, and walked back to the car. "Fine. Stay if you like, but try to stay out of people's affairs, okay? We don't like that around here."

I nodded once. The mayor pulled out of the lot. I took a drink of my cola.

"She seems nice." Bozeman said. I'm surprised the mayor didn't notice him standing just inside the bus door, but then again, I was so used to his presence, I always sensed when he was around.

"Yeah, she's a peach," I said.

"You mind if I come out there and do some writing?" Bozeman asked.

"Of course not. There's plenty of room for you."

Bozeman stepped from the bus carrying a guitar in one hand and a notebook in the other. He sat in the other chair and opened the notebook to the tune he was working on. He started experimenting with different melodies and runs, trying to find the perfect sound for his new song. I picked the book back up and started again on page one.

I must have fallen asleep at some point, because I heard Bozeman calling my name.

"What?"

He pointed at me. "Your pocket's buzzing."

I had forgotten about the phone. I fished it from my pocket and accepted the call without looking to see who it was.

"Hello?"

"Codi Cassidy?" The voice sounded familiar, but I didn't know for sure who it was.

"I know who killed Sherman Stier, and I have evidence. I saw who did it. Are you interested?"

I sat up straight and came to attention. "Of course. Who is this?"

"This is someone who has the information you want."

"Why don't you go to the police? Take your evidence to the chief?" That seemed logical to me.

There was a pause on the other end of the line. "I can't trust the chief. You shouldn't either. There are many people in this town you shouldn't trust for a lot of reasons, especially Sam Henry."

Now it was my turn for the pause. "Are you saying there's a conspiracy going on? That this is about more than a grudge against Sherman Stier?"

"Maybe," the voice said.

"Why come to me? If you don't trust the chief, why not call in the state police, or go to the mayor?"

"Can't trust the mayor either. And you're already here. Sometimes you have to bring in an outside exterminator to remove the rats. I won't say anymore over the phone. Meet me at the flower shop at two."

The line dropped dead.

Bozeman looked over at me. "What was all that about?"

"Beats me. It's someone claiming to have information about the murder. The mayor was right about one thing. We should have left town last night. I'll be right back."

I got up and walked around the building to Sam's apartment entrance. She locked the street level door, so I rang the bell and waited. Sam didn't answer, so I hit the bell several times in quick succession and stood on the street, waiting for Sam to appear. She didn't. I took a step back and yelled up at the window for her, but got no response.

I stepped over to the bakery and tried the door, but she had locked that too. I looked through the window, and everything looked buttoned up. The chairs were on top of the table like someone had recently washed the floor, and the empty display case gleamed. I moved to the rear of the bakery and tried the back door. Locked. I knocked on the door but got no response. I thought I heard something inside, so I put my ear to the door and listened. All was quiet again.

I fished out my phone and found Sam's number. She didn't answer, so I waited for the voice greeting to finish and left a message. "Hey Sam, it's Codi. I got a strange call, I suspect, from Hanson. He says he has information about the murder, and we're supposed to meet him at the flower shop at two. Call me back or come out to the bus when you get this message."

I hung up and headed back to my chair. Bozeman stopped strumming and gave me a look.

"She's not there. Although she told me earlier she hadn't

slept all night, so she's probably napping," I said.

"Through all that racket? I heard you banging on the door and shouting for her from here. She must be a deep sleeper."

I checked the time on the phone. I still had a few hours to wait until two, and I guessed those hours would creep along.

At two o'clock, I tried rousing Sam, but again, I got no answer to my in-person visit or my phone calls. Since I was already late, I rushed over to the flower shop and stood outside on the sidewalk, only to find the door locked and the shop dark. Was I too late? I stood outside for fifteen minutes and tried to decide if I should write the phone call off as a prank, or if there was something else I should do. I ran with something else. The bakery had a back door, so I imagined the flower shop did as well.

I walked down Main Street to the end of the block, turned the corner, and ducked into the alley. I followed the alley until I came to the back door of the flower shop. Hanson's delivery van stood outside, and as I walked closer to the building, I noticed the door was ajar.

I pushed the door open wide and stepped across the threshold. "Hanson? Are you here? It's Codi. You called me this morning. I'm here."

The room was dark, so I checked the wall, discovered a light switch, and flipped it up. "Hanson?"

The back room of the flower shop was a mess. There was a large table with old plant clippings on it. An overflowing trash can was stuffed with greenery and wilted flowers stood to my left. There were flower boxes, vases, containers, and floral supplies everywhere. I took another step and discovered an open box filled with the centerpieces from the previous night. There was a doorway ahead, and I walked through that and found myself in the shop's front. The front was a complete opposite from the back. While the back was a mess of disorganization mixed with trash, the front was neat and organized. There was enough sunlight streaming through the large front window to see, so I walked quickly around the space to see if I could see anyone. Nothing.

I returned to the back room and to my right I noticed a walk-in refrigerator, much like I had seen at the diner. This unit had a small window in the door, so I got on my tiptoes and looked inside. From what I could tell, Hanson filled it with shelving units and flowers. I tugged open the heavy door for a better look. The first thing that caught my attention was the overwhelming smell of roses. The second thing was the body on the floor.

I closed the door, made an extremely hasty exit, and called the police.

Twenty minutes later, I was sitting on an overturned crate in the alley when Chief Jennings came out of the building.

The chief removed his hat, wiped his brow, and returned the hat to his head. "Yep, that's Hanson Johns in there. You want to tell me why you were here?"

The words 'you can't trust the chief' echoed through my head as I got the story together in my head. I didn't know where that fine line was between telling him everything I had to holding things back and having them potentially used against me later.

"He called me and asked me to meet him out front at two. When the time passed, I came around here, found the door ajar, and found him where you did."

"Did you touch the body?"

"No. I came right outside and called you guys."

Chief Jennings got out his ever-present notepad and wrote something down.

"Why did he want to meet with you?"

"He said he had information about Sherman Stier's death."

"So why call you, and not me, then?"

That was the question, wasn't it? Why indeed? "He knew I'm Sam's friend. I think he had information to clear her. He said he witnessed the murder."

Chief Jennings stared at me. I couldn't tell if he believed me or not.

"Did he leave you a message, or did you speak to him directly?"

"I talked to him."

"Can I have your phone, please?"

I dug it out of my pocket and held it out to him.

"You got a lock code on there?"

I shook my head no.

The chief took the phone from me and called a deputy over and handed him my cell. "Samuels, get the numbers of any calls incoming or outgoing for today only, and get this right back to me. I'll be right back."

I watched as an ambulance pulled into the alley and the two paramedics exited the ambulance and talked to the chief. The door opened, and they wheeled a gurney into the flower shop. A few minutes later, they returned, loaded the sheet-covered body into the back, and left without lights or sirens.

A few minutes later, I saw Samuels give something to Jennings, and then the chief came back to me.

"You can have your phone back. The one incoming call was probably a burner number. Care to tell me about the fifteen calls you made to Sam Henry?"

That was the question I feared would come up. I told him how we got together for breakfast, and how she went to bed afterward, and I explained about how I tried to contact her multiple times after Hanson called me. I couldn't tell if I convinced him it was the truth or not.

"Am I a suspect here?" I wanted to be as blunt as possible, and I wanted to know if I needed to bring in a lawyer.

"Did you touch anything inside the building?"

I hated it when people answered questions with questions. I thought for a moment. "Let's see. I pushed the back door open. Then I turned on the light by the door, and I opened the refrigerator. I think that was it."

"Nothing else? You didn't handle the cash register? Or pick anything up, or lean on any surfaces?"

Did I? I was certain I didn't go near the register or handle anything. "No. I don't think so."

"Do you mind if we take your fingerprints? We'll get them eventually, so you can provide them now, or we can take you to the station for a more formal questioning."

I wasn't one for formalities, and I knew they'd get them sooner rather than later. "You can have them now."

Chief Jennings called Samuels back over. "Get her fingerprints, will you?"

I held out my hand, expecting my fingertips to be dipped in ink.

Samuels shook his head. "We don't do it that way anymore, ma'am. Can you touch the screen?"

I looked down and saw Samuels had a device just a little larger than my cell phone. "What's that thing?"

Samuels smiled. "Portable ID unit. Scans all ten of your fingerprints right into the database."

"You have any outstanding warrants you want to tell me about?" Chief Jennings asked. "As soon as the prints hit the database, a search will start and will find out if you do."

"No. Not even an outstanding speeding ticket." At last, a simple question I could answer.

A few seconds later, Samuels got a beep from his phone and checked the message. "She's clean."

"Thanks." Jennings dismissed Samuels again, and Samuels returned to the flower shop.

Jennings turned his attention back to me. "You know, this is usually a nice, quiet town. Occasionally we'll get some knuckleheads drag racing through downtown, or we'll have to break up an underage drinking party. We get a fair amount of speeding tickets from the tourists who think the state highway has the same speed limit as the interstate. And of course, there's a bit of petty theft that happens at the market, but usually, it's pretty tranquil around here. And then you showed up and we've had two murders in as many days. What would you call that?"

I looked up at him. "An unlucky coincidence?"

"Don't leave town until I say you can go. No matter what the mayor says. I'm done with you for now. You can go on back to your bus."

I didn't hesitate for a moment. As I got to the alley's end, I noticed a small crowd had accumulated just outside the crime scene tape barrier the police had erected. I didn't recognize anyone. I ducked under the tape and made a beeline for the bus.

Where was Sam? Why hadn't she returned my calls? I didn't know if I was madder at her for ignoring me, or more concerned that something had happened to her, too. I needed to talk to Sam, so rather than return to the bus like I initially intended, I switched direction and stepped to her door instead. Still locked. I rang the bell.

A few seconds later, Sam appeared above me. "Hey, you."

I glared up at her. "Hey yourself. Get down here and let me in. We need to talk."

CHAPTER TEN

I waited a minute for Sam to come down and unlock the door, and then I followed her back up to her apartment. She sat on the couch while I paced back and forth in her living room.

"Where have you been? I called you like a thousand times."

"I took a nap. Look, I'm sorry, I said it would be a couple hours, but I was afraid I wouldn't be able to sleep, so I took a pill. Afterward, I dropped off like the dead."

"Poor choice of words. The florist is dead. I found him."

Sam looked stunned. "Hanson? Dead? What do you mean? I don't understand."

"I found him in the flower shop, in the fridge with the flowers."

"That's horrible!" Sam stood and came over to hug me. I didn't want to accept it at first, but I eventually let her put her arms around me. I admit, it felt comforting.

"Are you okay?" Sam took me by the hand and led me to the couch. We both sat.

"Yes. No. I don't know," I said.

"What were you doing at the flower shop in the first place?"

Sam asked.

"That's why I've been trying to get a hold of you. Hanson called me and told me he had an idea who killed Sherman, and I was supposed to meet him at the shop at two. I was going to get you to meet him with me, but you didn't answer the doorbell or the phone, so I headed over there by myself. The back door was open, so I entered the shop, and when I opened the fridge, there he was on the floor."

"Oh, my. What happened?"

"Well, I called the police, and they came over and questioned me and took the body away."

"I don't believe it. Do you know how he died?" Sam asked.

I shook my head. "No. I only saw his legs, and that was enough for me."

"What about the evidence of who killed Sherman? Did you find anything there about that? Anything that would clear me?"

I shook my head again. Evidence? Had I said anything about Hanson having evidence? I couldn't think straight. The experience had scrambled my brain.

Sam leaned back in her seat and rubbed her eyes. "So now what do we do?"

I didn't really know. I felt like I was past the point of getting in over my head, and what I wanted to do most was get on the bus and head off to California for our next gig. But unfortunately, I had given Sam my word to help her out, and I hardly ever went back on my word.

"Your guess is as good as mine. I was certain someone from the committee did Sherman in, and I have to admit, when Hanson called and said he had the answer, my heart flipped with excitement. I'm so ready to put all this behind us. We've cleared the McMurtrys and Reba. Obviously, Hanson didn't do it unless there was a second killer out there somewhere. You didn't do it, did you? If you did, I've solved the mystery," I said.

I looked over at Sam, and finally, a smile appeared on her face. "No. I didn't do it. Did you?"

"I did not. So we can cross our names off the list. Bozeman didn't do it. I can vouch for him. Who does that leave? Dean Williams? Pastor Tom? Mayor Mary? Someone I never even considered? There were, what, a couple hundred people there last night? Any of them might have stabbed Sherman. And there wouldn't have to be a real motive. Maybe Sherman skipped someone in line, or stole a parking space. We live in nutty times, and people kill for nutty reasons."

"Yeah, but we don't have that kind of oddness around these parts. This is a pretty quiet little city," Sam said.

"I've been told that by the chief and the mayor."

We stayed silent for a few moments, each of us gathering our own thoughts.

"What about Harold Johns?" Sam asked.

"Hanson's brother?" I asked.

"Yes. I heard he was upset when the resort was first proposed. Said it would affect business at the hotel. And rumor has it he's already upside down on the property, so any change in business would end him."

I mulled it over for a moment. "Sure, that's a plausible motive, but Hanson told me last night that Harold is out of town, helping his folks. Is that true? When's the last time anyone talked to him?"

Sam let loose a long exhale. "That's right. He used to come into the bakery at least twice a week, but I haven't seen him in at least a couple of months. And I imagine they will confirm his story the second the police call Hanson's next of kin to report his death."

"True," I said.

"What about a hitman? Did someone hire some muscle to take care of Sherman, and then Hanson, to tie up loose ends?" Sam asked.

"If this were a large city, I'd say it was at least possible, but here, in Quincey, New Mexico? I doubt it. I'm sure people would notice a stranger in town. Heck, just yesterday I was a stranger in town, and you can't imagine all the looks I got from people when I was walking around before you found me. I got stares at the restaurant last night, and this morning. Small town folks seem to have a radar that alerts on people who aren't from here. Besides, did you see anyone at the event last night that you didn't recognize?"

Sam responded almost right away. "Well, no."

"Exactly. If a hired gun had come in and stabbed Sherman, I'm one hundred percent sure that someone would have remembered the person and reported it."

Sam nodded. "You're right. They would've stood out like a purple duck. Do you really think Pastor Tom might be in on it?"

I looked at her, then at my shoes. "You got me. I get he's a man of the cloth and all, but when I was talking to him last night, he seemed evasive about his relationship with Sherman. He gave me the impression that Sherman had donated a lot of money to the church. I can't figure out why he would, though."

"Maybe he was just doing a good deed? Like with improving the fire station?"

I shook my head and frowned. "No, I don't think so. If you build a new fire station, that benefits you if there's a fire. How does giving a chunk of cash to the church help Sherman? From what I've gathered, he's not the type of guy to offer something just because of the goodness in his heart."

"True. You want to go back to the church and talk to the pastor?"

"Why don't we wait until tomorrow for that visit? I would imagine Sunday is his busy day."

Sam laughed. "Yes. Of course, it is. I'd forgotten it's only Sunday. What makes you think the mayor's involved?"

I glanced over at Sam. "She came over for a visit this morning."

"No! What did she want?"

"The long and short of it was she invited me to hit the road at my earliest convenience," I said.

"But doesn't Chief Jennings want you to stick around?" Sam asked.

"He does. She gave me her advice before I found poor Hanson. Anyway, I don't think she stabbed Sherman herself, but I have a suspicion she's indirectly involved somehow."

"Why?"

"Oh, just a feeling, mostly. I also found it odd that business owners around town have brought their resort concerns to her attention, and what has she done about them all?"

"Well, nothing that I'm aware of. In short, she told us all about a month ago to bugger off about the resort completely."

"And that didn't strike you as odd?" I asked.

"Now that you bring it up, it does. Why would she so willingly side with an outsider to the detriment of the townies?"

"Exactly. So, either she's involved in something shady, and she had to get rid of Sherman. Or she's involved in something shady and was in league with Sherman. Either way."

"Or she might be completely innocent."

"Sure, Sam, perhaps she is. But I'd bet my favorite pair of boots that there's something going on there. And that leads me right back to Dean."

I looked over at Sam, who caught my gaze, then jumped up from the couch and headed for the kitchen. "You want anything to drink? I'm getting a root beer."

"Sounds good to me." I listened to the fridge open and close, followed by the sounds of Sam retrieving glasses from the cabinet. I picked up the sound of the pop top snap, and the familiar glug-glug sound of root beer falling into a glass. A few seconds later, she was back.

"Sorry, I don't have any ice." She held out a glass, and I took it. We touched glasses in a mock toast and drank. It was good. I couldn't remember the last time I had a root beer.

I hesitated, but I had to broach the subject again, and I assumed to Sam it was like a scab being picked at until it bled.

"So, Dean Williams."

Sam drained half her glass, then set it on the table beside her and looked at me. "I know, I know. You think he's the most likely suspect, right?"

I nodded.

"Why?"

I set my glass down and counted the points on my fingers. "First, he seems overprotective of you. Second, looking in from the outside, he appears to have anger issues. Third, he had an opportunity. You told me yourself he was right there just after you came out of the bathroom and just before you found the body, right? Fourth, I overheard him on more than one occasion talking about 'dealing with Sherman', and who knows what he meant there?" I dropped my hands and picked my glass back up. "Sorry to be blunt. I understand he's a friend."

"No. It's okay. That's one reason I asked for your help. I'm too close to this. I appreciate your fresh set of eyes on everything around here. Still friends?"

I smiled. "Of course. What's a little murder between buddies?"

We both laughed, and the tension washed away. I felt better, more relaxed. I didn't realize that I had built up enough internal pressure to run a V8 engine.

"Hey, what do you say—"

The doorbell interrupted Sam. She crossed over to the window and looked outside. "It's Shanna. Shanna, come on up, the door's unlocked."

Sam moved over to the apartment door, opened it, and soon Shanna stepped through.

I noticed Shanna had been crying. Her eyes were red and puffy and there was a faint black line on the side of her face where she'd tried to wipe away a streak of mascara. Sam noticed it, too.

"What's wrong? What happened?" Sam asked.

Shanna sniffed and gulped some air. "When I got home, I found this."

Shanna lifted her arm, and I saw in her right hand a plastic sandwich bag, and within that bag was an index card. She turned it around so we could read it. We both saw the words 'you're next' in big block letters in red ink.

I saw the note, then sat back down. Things were getting unreal. "Tell me everything about finding that," I said.

Shanna sniffed again. Sam motioned for her to sit on the easy chair and then passed her a box of tissues. Shanna grabbed a tissue, blew her nose, and took a breath. "I was at the gym. I go every Sunday to an afternoon yoga class. When I got home, I noticed this lying on the living room floor. I figured it was a coupon or something because people were always sliding things under my door, but when I turned it over, I saw that. I remembered what happened to Sherman Stier, and I got scared."

Sam and I looked at each other.

"Did you call the police?" I asked.

"Do you think I should?"

"Without a doubt. There's more going on here than you know. Here's what you should do. Go home, call Chief Jennings, and tell them exactly what you found and how you found it."

"I can't call from here?"

"You may, but the police would want to see where it happened, so you'd have to go home, anyway."

"Okay. If you say that's best."

Sam gave Shanna a hug. "It probably is best that way. If you need us, we'll be here."

Shanna sniffed again. "Should I tell the chief I came here?"

Sam and I looked at each other again, but it was me who spoke first. "If it were me, I wouldn't bring it up. But, if you're asked if you went anywhere between the time you found it and the time you called them, tell them. It's important that you don't lie. Okay?"

Shanna slowly nodded. "Okay. Thank you."

Shanna got to her feet and took another tissue from the box.

"I'll call you later, okay?" Shanna said.

Sam ushered Shanna from the room and walked her down the stairs. I heard voices from the open window, but I didn't hear what they were saying. A few minutes later, Sam returned.

"Well?" she asked.

I drank some root beer and set down the glass. "Can this day get any more complicated?"

Sam exhaled. "I sure hope not. What do we do now? Do you want to find someone else to talk to, or should we wait and see what happens with Shanna?"

"Well, we said we'd be here, so I guess we should settle in for a bit."

We didn't know how long it would take for Shanna to call, so we found things to occupy our time. The first hour we spent talking about old times and gossiping about people we remembered from high school. Of course, I had to provide most of the information since I had a few dozen of them as followers of my social media.

After we ran out of people to talk about, we dove into a few magazines that Sam had lying around the house. Shortly after seven, Sam dug out a deck of cards and we played a rousing round of Go Fish, followed by a couple of games of War. Just as Sam's cat clock slipped into the eight o'clock hour, we finally heard heavy footsteps ascending the stairs.

A hard knock fell upon the door. "Quincey Police Department. Open up. We have a warrant."

Sam and I passed confused glances, and she moved to the door and opened it. As she did, two deputies rushed into the room with guns drawn. One deputy motioned for Sam to join me on the couch, while the other did a sweep of the tiny apartment.

"All clear," the second deputy said as he joined the other one.

Sam didn't look well, and she started shaking. I put an arm around her and tried to steady her. "What's this about a warrant?" Sam asked.

Chief Jennings entered the room and stepped forward,

offering Sam a sheet of paper. "Samantha Henry, I have a warrant for your arrest for the murders of Sherman Stier and Hanson Johns, and for making terroristic threats to Shanna Prescott. Please stand and put your arms behind your back."

Sam shook her head back and forth with such force I expected it to pop off and roll across the floor like a bowling ball.

"No. I didn't do it. I didn't do any of those things. You need to listen to me!" she screamed.

A deputy reached forward and grabbed Sam's upper arm. Sam responded by trying to become one with the couch. "No! Stop! I'm innocent!"

The other deputy stepped in, and between the two of them, they got Sam to her feet, spun her around, and slapped handcuffs on her. After that, Chief Jennings stepped over and patted her down for weapons.

"I'll bet you loved that, you pig!" Sam snarled. "You've always wanted to get your hands on me! Let me go! I didn't do any of those things!" Sam broke and the tears flowed. She looked in my direction and muttered something. I couldn't tell what it was, and before I asked for clarification, the deputies escorted her from the room.

The chief started looking around the room. I stood and followed him into the kitchen.

"What are you doing?"

"I'm executing a warrant, looking for evidence."

"I don't think —"

Chief Jennings spun around. "Look, I've had about enough of you. You should leave before I charge you as an accessory to her crimes."

"There's no way. You can't. You don't have any evidence."

The chief threw me a sly smile. "Not to worry. I'm sure I could come up with something. Go back to your bus. Relax, have a nice evening, and then tomorrow, leave Quincey. Do us a favor and don't come back."

"No. You can't run me off, and you have nothing on Sam.

You should let her go."

Before the chief could say anything, Deputy Samuels appeared in the kitchen carrying two small evidence bags and handed them to Jennings. "Got them. They look like they match to me."

"Thanks. Search the other rooms up here." Chief Jennings turned back to me and held the evidence bags directly in front of my face. "No evidence? See these?"

I tried to focus on what he had, but they were so close to my face I couldn't make out either item. After I moved my head back, and they came into view. I saw what they were, but I didn't know the relevancy. "Yeah? So what?"

"So what? She stabbed Sherman Stier with one of her own knives. Has her name on the handle, along with her fingerprints. She killed Hanson Johns with a pie cutter, one that looks just like this." Chief Jennings showed the bag with the pie cutter in it. "And she wrote the threat against Shanna on a card, exactly like the card like this that Sam writes recipes on. We've also found her fingerprints at the scene of each crime."

It all was hard for me to process. I was about to argue with him about being her alibi, but I realized I couldn't. Sure, I was with her at breakfast, and several people saw us then. And I was with her later in the afternoon, but that left a sizeable gap of time when I couldn't get in touch with her. Since the police already had my outgoing phone call log, they knew that. We'd been apart for about six hours. It was certainly enough time to off the flower man and leave a note under a door. Despite that, I believed my friend wasn't capable of such things.

The chief looked indignant and appeared to be waiting for me to say something. "Well?"

I coughed, then shook my head. "Look, I'm sorry, Chief Jennings, I didn't mean to come across as so aggressive. I'm just in shock, is all."

The chief must have taken my word for once because his shoulders slumped, and he slid into a more relaxed posture.

"Do you think I can see her? Please? I just want to make sure she's okay and that she at least has a lawyer. Would that be okay?"

The chief stared at me long enough for me to wonder if I had not said the words out loud.

"Yeah. Okay. But not tonight. It's already late, and she needs to go through processing. Tomorrow morning, come down to the jail and I'll make sure you can talk to her. Come early though, because we don't have a long-term facility, so we'll send her to the county jail in the afternoon."

I nodded. "I understand. Thank you, Chief Jennings."

It was time to leave.

"Cassidy?"

"Yes, Chief?"

"Don't do or say anything stupid. You've worn out your welcome here."

Without a word, I left the apartment, walked around the building, and entered the bus. Bozeman was in the kitchen making a snack. "Want a sandwich? Ham and cheese?"

My stomach rumbled. It was a busy day, and I hadn't eaten since breakfast. "I'd love one, thanks."

"Hot or cold?"

I smiled. I loved grilled ham and cheese. "Hot. Please."

Bozeman took a couple of extra slices from the bread, buttered a side of each, and slid them into the pan next to his. Bozeman was a chef of contradiction. He couldn't make a decent fried egg, but he could make a delicious sandwich. Give him a steak and every time it would turn out like jerky. Hand him a fish, and it would turn out flaky and delicate. I didn't understand it, but I had learned to work around it. If he was making a food he'd mastered, I'd always accept his offer for the meal. If it was something he couldn't cook right to save his life, I'd cook either just for myself or for both of us. Between the two of us, we got by fine at mealtimes.

"Where have you been all day? I thought you'd be right

back."

I removed my baseball cap, tossed it on the chair, and ran my fingers through my hair. "You would not believe everything that happened today."

"Did you clear your friend of the murder?"

"Actually, I got her indicted in a second one. Oh, and accused of making a terroristic threat, whatever that is."

Bozeman turned around to face me, spatula in hand. "You're kidding."

I shook my head and frowned. I wanted to run to my room and cry or hide. But I also wanted the sandwich, so I sat tight. Gibson must have sensed my discomfort as he jumped up into my lap and nuzzled my chin. I giggled. "Hey, little man, your nose is cold and wet."

A few minutes later, Bozeman slid a plate in front of me and sat down across from me. Gibson moved to the seat next to me and laid his head on my leg while Bozeman and I ate in silence, which I was grateful for. After we finished the meal, I dumped the paper plates into the trash, washed Bozeman's pan, and rejoined him at the table.

"So, tell me about your day," he said.

CHAPTER ELEVEN

I didn't imagine I'd sleep that night, but I did, and I was glad about it. I woke up refreshed and ready to take on the day. Bozeman was still asleep, so I fed the animals and made myself a cup of tea. Every day I make a mental list of the things I wanted to accomplish during the day, and today's list comprised only two items. Find out who really committed two murders and get Sam out of jail. Easy peasy, squeezy lemon.

Around nine, I was ready to go, so I used my phone to find the directions to the local jail. To my dismay, it was over a mile away. I didn't have the heart to wake Bozeman to drive me over, and there didn't appear to be any ride share options in the area. So, I put on my most comfortable pair of sneakers and headed out for a walk.

I'm not a fast walker, partially because I'm so short, but mostly because I like to look at stuff as I go. Since I knew this morning I was on a mission, it took everything I had not to stop at a park I passed and sit on a bench and watch the birds. I had more important things to do, and I knew I needed to stay on task. That part wasn't easy, either, since I lived a non-structured lifestyle. Every day wasn't like the normal every day of the people who had to work nine-to-five jobs. I appreciated that, although I often let my thoughts wander, and sometimes didn't get the tasks done I wanted to do for the day. Today was different, though. Sam was depending on me, and I had to come through for her.

Around nine-thirty, I strode into the local jail. It was a small building that looked fairly new, and I wondered if Sherman Stier had put up the money for this one as well. I approached the desk and was about to explain what I needed when Deputy Samuels opened an inner door and motioned for me to follow him through.

"You have any weapons on you? Gun, knife?" he asked as he ushered me into an interview room.

I was glad for once I had left Betty behind. "No."

"Sam will be right in. Usually, we don't let friends or family talk to the prisoners, so we're breaking the rules for you here."

"I appreciate that, Deputy. Thank you."

Samuels dropped his voice to a whisper. "Thank you for helping her. I like Sam, I really do, and I can't imagine she did these horrible things. But I can't let my personal feelings impede following the law. You can understand that, right?"

I smiled and nodded.

Another deputy led Sam into the room and cuffed her hands to a metal ring on the table I hadn't noticed when I sat down.

"Knock on the door when you're ready to leave," Samuels said. "There's also a camera in the upper corner of this room, so we will record you since you're not an attorney. There's nothing I can do about that. Got it?"

I nodded again. "Crystal clear. Thank you again."

Deputy Samuels closed the door, and the second it shut, I stood and gave Sam a hug.

"You look horrible in orange," I said.

Sam gave me a weak smile. "Everyone does. At least I don't have to wear the black-and-white striped outfit. That would be really embarrassing."

"How are they treating you in here? What's happened?"

Sam leaned over and ran her fingers through her unkempt hair. "It's not as bad as I pictured. I'm the only woman in here, so they gave me a cell of my own. I got fingerprinted, and my pictures taken, and they tried to ask me questions, but I said I wouldn't say anything until my lawyer got here."

"Do you have a lawyer? Do I need to get you one?"

Sam shook her head. "No, I'm good. I have a business lawyer on retainer for the bakery, and she's tracking down one who can handle the criminal charges. Should be here later this morning. Hey, Chief Jennings told me he told you about the evidence they have against me. I know it looks bad, but believe me, Codi, I didn't do any of it. I couldn't have."

Without being obvious, I glanced up at the camera. I half-expected it to be discreet so that you'd not notice it was there, or perhaps hidden behind one-way glass like in the movies. But no, it looked like a relic from the 1990s, and was out there in full view of anyone in the room. I couldn't decide if I should risk asking her further questions, or if I should keep my plan to myself.

"Sam, I believe you. I assumed you didn't do any of those things," I said.

"Can you do me a favor?" Sam asked.

"Sure. What?"

"Can you contact Dean for me and tell him where I am? He'll be worried about me, and I really don't want him to go off and do anything stupid. Sometimes he specializes in stupid."

"Sure thing." I didn't say it, but Dean was my next stop after this visit was over. He was still number one on my suspect list, and now that they had Sam behind bars, I hoped to use that pressure against him. If he really cared about her, perhaps he'd finally crack.

"Where can I find him?" I asked.

"After ten, he should be at the museum. Do you remember where that is? On Main Street, between the diner and the bakery?"

"I remember seeing it, so I should be able to find it. If not, I can look it up on my phone."

"Thank you."

I smiled. "Anything else?"

Sam was silent for a moment.

"What are you daydreaming about?" I asked.

She looked up at me. "My bakery. It's already past opening time. I can picture the people coming by for their daily bread and not being able to get it. And the McMurtrys. What are they going to do at the diner?"

Sam tried to remain strong, but cried. "This will ruin me here. I'll lose the diner contract with the McMurtrys, and this will shoot my reputation right between the eyes. People talk around here. I'll have to close the doors. I can't afford to start over. Not anymore. I can't do this."

I reached for her, held her close, and let her sob into my second favorite shirt. "It'll be okay. I'll stop by the diner on the way to visit Dean and explain things to Rob and Lisa, okay?"

"Okay."

"Could Shanna run the bakery while you're gone? Only to keep things going?"

Sam shook her head. "No, she's not ready. There's just so much to do."

"Can she at least let me in? We could put a sign on the window that says you're on vacation or something."

Sam's sobs turned to sniffles, so I let her loose and retook my seat.

"No. I locked the bakery, and the key is on my key chain. The police have that."

"Okay. Look, Sam, I haven't given up on you. We'll figure this out. Just give me a little time."

Sam nodded.

"Need anything else?"

"Yeah, could you break into the bakery and bake me a cake

with a file in it?"

The statement gave me pause, then Sam gave a hesitant laugh, and I followed suit. The police had restricted her freedom, but hadn't constrained her odd sense of humor. I guess that was a good thing.

"It would taste like crap, but I could do it." I gave Sam a last hug, then knocked on the door. After a few seconds, a deputy let me out, and I walked through the police station and stepped out into the sunshine. Weather-wise, it looked to be a beautiful day. I hoped Sam would be out in time to watch the sunset. I exhaled and started walking toward downtown.

Twenty minutes later, I stepped into the busy diner. I must have missed the Monday morning breakfast rush because there were only two tables taken when I got there. I spotted Lisa when I entered the door, begged her for a glass of water, and explained as much of Sam's situation as I could without going into too many details. She seemed to understand. To my delight, she gave me her assurances that she and Rob would both stick by Sam through thick or thin, and I left the diner, relieved the conversation had gone so well.

It was the next talk I wasn't looking forward to.

It wasn't a far walk from the diner to the museum, but it seemed to take me twice as long to make that journey as it had from the bus to the jail.

The opening hour was ten, and I checked my phone and it was half past, so I tugged on the door, which opened freely, and I stepped into the building.

I had no expectations when I walked into the Quincey Museum of Local History. But I got a pleasant surprise when I passed through the door and stepped back into the 1800s.

The front admission desk looked like it came right from an old bank. The desk itself was about six feet wide, and below the waist, an artisan had carved an ornate pattern into it. Above the waist, there were three windows with ornate vertical brass bars and a small area below to pass items. Above the window was a sign with the word Teller spelled out in brass letters.

"Can I help you?" I noticed the person behind the window was a woman who looked to be in her early twenties. She dressed like I'd expect a male bank teller to be dressed, right down to the shiny vest and black tie. She even sported the visor I'd associate with the times.

"Yes. I'm here to talk to Dean Williams. Is he available?"

The teller picked up the phone and dialed a number. "There's a woman here to see you. Yes, she's short. Blue hair?"

I lifted my ball cap so she could check out the color underneath.

"Yes. She has blue hair. Okay." The teller hung up the phone and pointed down the hallway. "He was expecting you. Go through the exhibit. At the end of the first section, you'll notice a hallway with a sign that says genealogy. He's in that room doing research."

I put my hat back on. "Thanks."

I strolled through the room, impressed by what I saw. The museum had recreated a street scene of what the town looked like a few years after its founding. It featured a dentist's office, a general store, a hotel that looked exactly like the Quincey Inn, and a lawyer's office. Each building had windows to see artifacts, and there were several information signs I wanted to stop and read, but I stayed on my mission.

Eventually, the street turned a corner to the right, and I spotted the hallway and found the genealogical library. That took my breath away, too. There was a wall lined with bookshelves that were stacked with all kinds of volumes. I spotted an old card catalog and several drawers that held tapes and microfiche. Against a wall stood a cabinet with drawers to accommodate large maps and two computer stations. In the center of the room, seated at a large table with three open books stacked around him, was Dean Williams.

He looked up from a tome and spotted me. "Come in. Sit down. Please."

I took a chair across from him.

His eyes dropped to the page, and without looking at me, he spoke. "I'd like to apologize for yesterday. I wasn't in my right mind, and I saw you as a threat, and now I realize you're just trying to help Sam."

"Apology accepted." I could be gracious. Sometimes.

He looked up and met my eyes. "I'd offer you a coffee or something, but there's no food or beverages allowed in this room. To protect the documents."

"I get it." And I did. At one time, I searched for leaves on my family tree and spent many hours in old libraries and the stacks of musty courthouses. I understood the rules. No food, no drink, no ink. "You have an impressive collection here."

"Yes. I've got the largest genealogical collection in this part of the state. I'm passionate about history, especially family history. A lot of the materials I've collected here are from closed libraries or from estate sales. I get donations from families as well who want to see their histories preserved. I've got records in here dating back to when this territory was still a part of Mexico."

"Impressive."

"So why are you here, Codi?"

"Did you know Hanson Johns is dead?"

Dean seemed interested in the book again and looked at the pages. He took a moment and wrote a note on a yellow legal pad beside him. "I heard that through the grapevine."

"Did you know they arrested Sam last night for both murders?"

That got his attention. He had been calm, but the fire I'd seen the night before passed behind his eyes. It quickly faded as he struggled to contain his anger.

"That I hadn't heard," he said.

I felt the need to press buttons since I was running short on time. "Do you believe she did it? Do you think she murdered two people in cold blood?"

"No, of course not," he said.

"Then who's your number one suspect? I can understand Hanson's murder if he saw who actually stabbed Sherman, but who, besides Sam, could hold the grudge enough to kill Sherman?"

Dean didn't say a word.

"You know, I really dislike the whole silent treatment thing. It's rude, and I'm confused by it. I thought you cared about Sam. Half the people I've talked to tell me you two are the hottest item in town, even though she denies it. Is she lying to me, Dean? Are you two a couple and for some strange reason, she doesn't want to tell me? Or is it the other way around? She's got the truth, and you're the one spreading lies around town about the two of you being together. Which is it? Tell me."

Dean exhaled and stared at me. He slammed the book closed, sprang from his seat, and carried the tome into the stacks. When he returned, his hands were empty. "Maybe it's time for you to leave."

I didn't move from the chair. "Maybe it's time you told me the truth."

He shook his head from side to side like a bull on the verge of rampaging. If he had anger issues like Sam said, perhaps I erred by not stopping back at the bus to pick up Bozeman, or better yet, Betty.

"You got something to say?" I asked. I guessed I was pressing my luck.

His chest puffed in and out as he breathed deep, but he remained where he was.

"Want to know what I think?" I asked.

"Not really," he said.

"I reckon you did it. You murdered two people and threatened Shanna, and you were the one who framed Sam to take the fall."

Dean took a step toward me. I stuck firm.

"Here's what I think happened, Dean-o. I think you did date Sam at one point, and I think she didn't care for the over-aggressive alpha male that you're displaying right now, so she dumped you. I bet you didn't handle that well and stalked her to possess her, if only in your own sick mind. Then Sherman came into the picture and pressed Sam to sell her bakery. You probably thought if you did the white knight routine and came to her rescue, then she'd change her mind. And you two would ride off into the sunset on your favorite horse. When Sherman threatened her with bodily harm last night, it was the final straw for you. So, you grabbed a knife from the kitchen, bull-rushed him into the pantry, and did the dirty deed. Unfortunately for poor Hanson, he soon came to the same conclusion I did, so you killed him too with the pie cutter you took from the church yesterday. How the note to Shanna figures in, I don't know, but the police can solve that piece. That sum everything up nicely for you, Dean?"

Dean took another step toward me, bent over, and screamed in my face. "I love her!"

I had enough, so I pushed the chair back and leaned toward him so close our eyebrows almost touched and screamed right back at him. "You love her so much she's going to get the death penalty for something you did?"

Dean made a move, and I thought he was going to hit me. Instead, he grabbed a book from the table and threw it across the room. It landed with a bang on top of a cabinet, then it slid across the surface and dropped to the floor. I wondered if he was going to toss me across the room next.

He clenched his teeth. "I wouldn't do that. You've got me all wrong. You don't understand."

"Everything okay in here?" Dean and I both looked at the door. The teller was standing there, her phone in hand, and she looked like she was ready to call for help.

Dean stepped back from me and smoothed out his shirt. "Yes, Amy. Everything is fine, just fine. We're just having a friendly discussion. You can go back to the front." Amy raised an eyebrow, paused for a moment, then left the room.

"Dean. Sit down. Please. Help me help Sam. If you love her,

do it."

Dean took a step for the door, then stopped. After a couple of seconds, he returned to his chair, and I took mine as well.

"Help me understand you. Come on. For Sam," I said.

He stared at the table surface, which was fine by me. "I know I'm out of control. There are… I've had some issues in the past, and I'm seeing a therapist about them. We're trying different medications, but we don't have the correct… balance yet. I love Sam, and I don't blame her for not wanting to be with me and my… dark side. But I didn't kill those people."

"Tell me what happened Saturday night when the fight started."

"Sherman was going to hit Sam, so I grabbed his arm. He tried to wrestle away from me, but I contained him for a moment. Then he let an elbow fly, and I caught it right in the face. See?"

Dean lifted his head and pointed. Right at the hairline was a bruise I hadn't noticed before. So much for my great powers of observation.

"After he whacked me, I relaxed my grip, and he slipped free, and followed Sam out the door. Of course, I was hot on his tail, but Rob intercepted me and dragged me into the kitchen and pushed me up against a counter and held me there."

"Did you try to get away from him?" I asked.

"Of course. But you've met the man. He's a giant. And he knows I go through these… spells, so he just held me there for like five minutes until I calmed down somewhat. Then he let me go."

"What did you do?"

"I needed some air, so I headed for the nearest door, almost knocked Sam over when she came out of the women's room. She looked okay, so I rushed outside, walked down the street like three or four blocks to clear my head, then slowly wandered back to the church. By then, they discovered Sherman's body."

"He was in the pantry. Did you see him in there? You walked right past it on your way out."

Dean thought for a moment. "No. I think the door was closed, and if it wasn't, I didn't notice. Sometimes I'm like a horse with blinders on, and I can only see what's directly in front of me."

"Where were you yesterday afternoon?"

"What? What are you talking about?"

"When someone killed Hanson."

Dean rose, stepped over to another desk, shuffled through some items, and returned carrying a sheet of paper. He handed it to me, and I glanced at it. "What's this for?"

"It's a receipt for some books I purchased at an estate sale yesterday around two. It was in Deming, which is a little over an hour from here. After the sale, I went out with a couple of guys for a bite to eat. I'm sure I can scrape up the receipt for that, too."

I dropped the paper on the table. He deflated my theory in an instant, like an old balloon. Now what?

"I can see why you thought it was me." Dean looked at the floor. "I'm sorry to disappoint you."

"Actually, I'm more disappointed, for Sam's sake. I'm almost out of ideas," I said.

Dean looked back at me. "If I were a betting man, I would've put my money on the mayor."

That got my attention. "What? Why the mayor?"

"Hold on."

Dean went to the map drawer and returned a few minutes later with a roll of paper and a couple of books. He found the end of the paper and placed a book on it, then unrolled the rest and set a book on the other end. I saw it was a map.

"This is a plat map of the Quincey and the surrounding areas. It's a little outdated by sixty or seventy years, but it'll work for this demonstration."

He looked around the area, found another book, and set it near the top of the map, then placed a second book right next to it. Then he extracted a dollar bill from his pocket and placed it along the bottom of the two books.

"Okay, look here. The books represent where the new resort will go. There are two proposed routes to get to that resort. The first is to the top, which is the main road that will run right through town on the county road and eventually feed into the interstate. The second route would cross right through that dollar bill, which would get to the interstate quicker and without going through town."

"So what?" I asked.

"The mayor currently owns that land and wants to sell it to the resort for a sizable amount of money, but Sherman's been blocking that sale."

"Let me guess. He's been stringing along the mayor until he got all the other improvements around the area he wanted."

"You got it. She's been having the planning commission rubber stamp practically everything he wants. Besides that, she's been tamping down all the complaints from the local businesses."

"I would imagine a direct feeder to the interstate would damage the local economy?"

"Some folks would be fine. I imagine there'd be a fast-food place or two and a gas station built at the brand-new exit. But if they did not force people through town, then they wouldn't know about the inn, or the diner, or this museum."

"You think the mayor killed Sherman so she can get his fellow investors to buy her land?"

Dean shrugged. "It's plausible."

"And that's the reason you're going to run against her?" I asked.

"Yes. I do genuinely care about this town and would prefer to see it thrive, rather than just the investors from other parts of the state."

"Now I understand why she was pushing me to leave town. Where would she be now?"

Dean rolled up the map and stacked the books in a neat pile. "At city hall. It's a couple of miles from here."

I exhaled. "Sounds like I should get walking, then. Thanks

for your time and all the clarifications."

I picked up my hat and left the room. I was outside the museum when someone tugged me on the arm. It was Dean.

"Come on, I'll drive you."

CHAPTER TWELVE

Dean's little green Honda stood right by the front door of the museum, so we got in, and he started the engine. Since I was used to riding high on the bus, as Dean sped up, it was like being in a go-cart for me. Dean made three consecutive right turns and a left, and we were back on Main Street, heading west. He seemed in a hurry. When we got to a stop sign and had to wait for a woman with a stroller to complete her long journey through the crosswalk, Dean showed his impatience by drumming his fingers on the steering wheel and shifting in his seat. Once she cleared the curb, Dean hit the accelerator, and I settled back into my seat like I was on an Apollo mission leaving Earth.

"Do you always drive like this?" I asked.

Dean glanced at me, and I snuck a peek at the speedometer. He was already going ten miles over the limit and getting faster.

"You told me you were in a hurry," he said.

"Not that much. Let me ask you, do you ever do nothing?" I asked.

"Nothing? What do you mean, nothing?"

"Like sitting outside and looking at the moon and stars?

Without thinking about anything and letting your mind clear out?"

"No, why?"

"Perhaps it would help you gain some focus. Maybe help you slow down a bit."

Dean slammed on the brakes, and as the momentum threw me forward in the seat, he turned a corner and stopped in a parking space with a final squeal of the tires. "We're here."

I considered walking back as I undid my seatbelt and left the car. Dean seemed to know the way, so I followed him into the building. It was a fairly new structure, two stories, rectangular, with the only splash of color being the United States and New Mexico flags waving in the wind out front. I assumed he'd been there before since Dean bypassed the information desk in front. He took an immediate left and started ascending the stairs to the second floor. Once at the top, he turned left again and followed the hallway to the end. At last, we stopped at the door to the mayor's office.

Dean held the door open for me and we stepped into the outer office. There was a receptionist's desk there, and although there was a steaming cup of coffee on it, there wasn't a person in sight. Dean took that as an invitation to go farther in. He stepped around the desk, rapped a knuckle on the inner door, peeked his head in, and opened the door wide.

If it surprised Mayor Mary to see us, she didn't show it. We walked into the room and stopped right in front of her desk. The mayor, who was reading a document, looked up at us over her glasses, exhaled, turned the document upside-down, and sat back in her large leather chair.

The mayor took off her reading glasses and dropped them on the desk. "What do you people want?"

I wanted to speak, but it was Dean who took the lead. Without asking or an invitation, he settled into the visitor's chair in front of her desk. "The sheriff arrested Sam Henry."

The mayor looked at him, at me, then back at him. "I already know that. He told me last night."

"She didn't do it," Dean said.

Mayor Mary shrugged her shoulders. "That's up for the court to decide, not you."

Dean stood suddenly and pointed his finger at the mayor's face and started screaming at her. "Look, Mary, we're all tired of you and your crap. I know you were involved, not Sam. You were the one who brought that weasel Stier to town, and you were the one who was looking to get rich while the rest of us suffered. I don't imagine things were going your way, so you got rid of him, didn't you? And you set Sam up to take the fall at the same time. Clever, Mary. Brilliant. Now that Stier's out of the way, I'm sure you've already started getting buddy-buddy with his investor friends, haven't you?"

Dean picked up the mayor's phone, held the receiver out to her, and lowered his voice to almost a whisper. "You need to get on this phone, call Chief Jennings, and get Sam out of jail. She doesn't belong there. You do."

The mayor didn't make a move, so Dean dropped the receiver. It landed on the desk with a thunk, then bounced and slipped off the side of the desk.

"Listen to me, you ass. I had nothing to do with the deaths of anyone. I didn't do it myself. I didn't have it done. You have no evidence to the contrary. Likewise, you have no evidence that I'm doing anything inappropriate regarding the new resort. You have nothing on me." The mayor leaned over, grabbed the phone's handset, and put it back on the base.

"We're done now. You can leave, either on your own, or I can get security to remove you. I'm happy either way."

Dean glared at her, and she glared right back. It was a contest of iron wills, and Dean broke first. Without a word, he got up, brushed past me, and left the office.

Mayor Mary looked at me. "Well?"

I gathered all the information I needed to. "I'll be leaving, I suppose. Have a nice day."

I left the office and retraced my steps back to the stairs and took them to the first floor. I assumed Dean would wait for me in the lobby, but he didn't. When I stepped outside, he wasn't there, either. I made my way to the parking lot, scanned all the spaces, and noticed his little green Honda was gone. Damn. There went my ride. I thought that was for the best.

I checked the map on my phone to make sure I had the directions right and started walking down Main Street. After fifteen minutes, I found myself in front of the police station, and I was happy to discover I was at least headed the right way. I continued down the street, not so much in a hurry anymore since I had run out of people to talk to. My suspect list had neat checkmarks next to every name, cleared completely, and I didn't know what to do. I'd run out of ideas.

As I walked, I overheard a church bell ring in the distance. Without thinking, I counted the peals in my head. It was noon, and since I had nothing for breakfast, I was hungry.

When I got to the diner, the lunch rush was on. Lisa spotted me, escorted me to the last table in the room, and handed me a menu.

"Want anything to drink, sweetie?" she asked.

I asked for water, and she scurried away to retrieve it while I glanced at the menu.

"I'd go with the meatloaf sandwich. They serve it open-faced with a side of mashed potatoes and gravy."

I looked over my menu and discovered it was Pastor Tom, offering his advice. "Do you mind if I join you? There's no other place to sit."

I used my foot to push a chair out for him. "Go ahead." As he sat, I returned to the menu. "The meatloaf wouldn't be too much food? I don't like being overstuffed."

"No. They serve it as a half-portion for lunch."

Lisa returned and dropped off glasses of water for me and the pastor. "Have you decided?"

I looked at the pastor. "I understand the meatloaf sandwich

is good. Let's try that."

"Same for me," Pastor Tom said.

Lisa scratched the order on her pad and left us.

I unwrapped a straw, sunk it into the water, and took a drink. The ice water tasted refreshing after the long walk I just took. "What's on your mind today, Pastor Tom?"

"My conscience, mostly. I saw Sam Henry at the jail today," the pastor said.

"Why were you there?"

"I go over there three times a week, talk to any inmate who wants to talk. Try to provide some comfort to them."

"Did you talk to Sam?" I asked. I took another drink. I'd almost drained my glass. Pastor Tom noticed and pushed his untouched one my way.

"Oh, yes."

"What did she say?"

"That she was innocent, but she feels like she's going to prison. She'll be one of those wrongfully convicted people you read about on the Internet. Her words, not mine," Pastor Tom said.

"Do you believe her? About being innocent?"

"Of murder? Yes, of course. She has fine Christian values."

That took me aback. "She didn't mention she attended your church."

Pastor Tom smiled at me. "No, I didn't say she was a good Christian. I said she had good Christian values. She doesn't attend my church, or any other church around town so far as I understand, but I see her at events, bake sales, Christmas programs, that sort of thing. What I meant to say was, she doesn't need to attend church to prove she's a good person, because she just is. She's generous with her time, and her humor. She bakes extra bread for the shelter, gives free cookies to the children, even makes a batch of dog treats once a week for any customers that have pooches. I've never seen her say an unkind word to anyone."

That sounded exactly like the Sam I remembered. "Except Sherman Stier?"

Pastor Tom got up and returned shortly with another glass of ice and a pitcher of water. He refilled my glasses, then poured himself one. Pastor Tom took a sip of water. "Well, that's a unique situation, isn't it? She was only fighting to protect what is hers, and we can't fault her for that, can we?"

I shook my head. After I took another drink, I dabbed my lips with a napkin.

"I can't wrap my head around this whole thing, Tom. I get Sam didn't do it, but I was so sure it was someone else from the committee who did. Lisa and Rob don't have a motive, and Dean Williams has an airtight alibi. Hanson is dead, and although I strongly suspect the mayor is up to some shenanigans, I don't think it's murder."

I looked up at him. "You didn't kill those men, did you?"

I thought I'd offended him. Instead, he broke into a hearty laugh. "Oh, my, no. It wasn't me."

"Sorry, Pastor, I had to ask. But you took some money from him, didn't you? I was right about that one?"

Pastor Tom frowned, then nodded. "Yes. One hundred and twenty-five thousand dollars. In cash. He handed it to me in a brown paper bag, like he was passing me a turkey sandwich."

"Why did he give you the money?" I asked.

The pastor swirled the straw in his glass as he thought for a moment. "One Saturday night I was working late, preparing the church for Sunday services, when he came in and plopped himself down in the back pew. As I got closer to him, I could tell he was drunk. His eyes were bloodshot, and he smelled like a distillery."

"What did he want?"

"He wanted to make a confession," the pastor said.

"A confession? You hear confessions?" I asked.

"Oh yes, all the time. I'm not Catholic, so I don't have the fancy confessional, or have people do Hail Marys or penance afterward, but I get confessions all the time. Sometimes people can't hold a secret, and the person they seek to tell is someone in the church. It comes with the position."

"And then you have to keep their secrets?"

"Oh yes. And I keep secrets much better than Reba Chestnut does, bless her."

We both laughed.

"And you keep everything in confidence? No matter what horrible thing they tell you?"

Pastor Tom took another drink. "No, not everything. If someone confesses to me about a crime against a person, I'll report that to the authorities."

"I thought that was against the rules."

"If I were a Roman-Catholic, it would be, because I would violate the seal of confession. But I have to look at it from the other perspective too. I can't stand by knowing that someone could have committed a rape, or assault, or even murder and not be accountable for it. In those cases, I would persuade the confessor to go to the authorities themselves, and if they didn't, I would."

"So, if I told you I stole a Snickers bar from the grocery store, you'd keep that secret, but if I shot the store clerk during the act, you would tell the cops?"

"Yes. That's right."

"I've never heard of that before."

"I believe I'm the exception, not the rule. Ah, here's lunch finally."

Lisa dropped off the food and left without another word. Pastor Tom bent his head and said a prayer, and although I wasn't really religious, I stayed silent as he did so to respect his beliefs. When he finished, we dug into our meals.

Pastor Tom had indeed made an excellent suggestion. The meatloaf was moist, seasoned properly and, in a word, excellent. It was so good; I ate three quarters of it, instead of my usual half. Then again, I had skipped breakfast, except for the tea. When I finished eating, I pushed my plate to the side.

"So Sherman Stier came in to confess about something. Since they didn't arrest him for anything, I assume that means he didn't confess to physically hurting anyone."

I looked over at Pastor Tom. He stayed silent, but he gave me a nearly imperceptible nod.

"Can you tell me what happened?" I asked.

Pastor Tom finished his meal, wiped his mouth with his napkin, then wiped up the crumbs on the table in front of him.

"He gave me his confession, begged me to keep his secret, and left in a hurry. A week later, he handed me a sack full of cash and told me to consider it a gift to the church for my help."

"He wanted to buy your silence."

"Yes. Although I would have kept his secret, anyway. I've heard much worse things during my time in the church."

"What are you going to do with the money?"

"I considered returning it to him, even recently, but now that he's gone, I suppose I'll keep it. That kind of money will go a long way to feeding the hungry and clothing the needy."

I couldn't find fault with that logic.

Pastor Tom rose suddenly. "Thank you for letting me join you for lunch. I have to run over to the retirement home. Don't worry about the check. I'll pick it up on the way out."

I smiled. "Thank you, that's quite kind."

Pastor Tom turned to leave, but came back, leaned close, and whispered in my ear. "You know, love is a strange thing. When people fall into it, they're so happy. When they fall out, sometimes they're sad, other times they're angry. Furious, even."

Pastor Tom stood, gave me a wink, and left me sitting by myself. I finished my water, left a tip for Lisa, and exited the diner.

I didn't have any place else I needed to go, so I jaywalked across the street, and did some window shopping as I ventured to the bus.

Our lawn chairs weren't outside, the area looked cleaned

up, and the door was locked tight, so I used my key to enter.

"Hello?" I said as I entered. "Anyone home?"

Silence greeted me, so I stepped over to the table and saw the note. Bozeman had gone for a run. Bozeman liked to keep active, and with our constant time spent on the road, he liked to use any downtime to exercise when he could. If we were in a town large enough to have the gym he had a nationwide membership for, he'd go there. If he didn't have that opportunity, he'd trade in his six-gallon hat and cowboy boots for a pair of shorts, a T-shirt, and running shoes. I had the place to myself.

There was a pile of black and white fur on the bench seat, curled up beneath the window, and although it could be mistaken for Gibson, I knew it was Merle. Merle lifted his head to watch me as I moved to the fridge and pulled a handful of raspberries from a pint.

"What are you doing up here? Fighting with your sister again?" Merle perked up when I sat next to him and waited for the treat he knew I would give him. First, though, I had to make sure the raspberries were nice and sweet, so I ate a couple myself. The little red morsels exploded in my mouth, and I moaned in delight.

"Want one?" I held one out for Merle, and like a gentleman, he took it in his front left foot and shoveled it into his mouth. He seemed to enjoy it as much as I did. I gave him my last raspberry, and he then crawled onto my lap and rolled over to get his belly scratched. My skunk was such a ham.

"Tell me, what's going on?" I knew he had gotten into a scuffle with Dolly. Although they loved each other most of the time, now and then they got into a minor argument, much like two dogs, or two cats, or two human siblings would do. When that happened, we usually brought either Merle or Dolly onto the bus, whoever was less grumpy at the moment, just to separate the two for a brief period. Obviously, a scuffle had ensued while I was gone, and Bozeman had to step in and be the mean parent.

"Where's your twin?" If I had to guess, Gibson was in his

usual spot on the pillow tower atop my bed. "You'll never believe the last couple of days I've been having. Every time I seem to have a handle on this thing, it just slips away from me again. So frustrating, you know?"

Merle raised his head. One would think he was paying attention. In reality, I knew he just wanted me to scratch the little white stripe that ran down his forehead between his cute black eyes. Merle has always been a diva.

"I'd better go see what your sister is up to. Do you want to go back downstairs?"

Merle answered that question by rolling off my lap and curling back into a ball on the cushion beside me. I took that as a no, so I rubbed his cute little ears and got up to go see what Dolly was up to.

I opened the door to Dolly's cage and glanced inside. As usual, Dolly had snuggled up in her blanket. Bozeman had given her a bowl of vegetables, but they didn't look touched.

"Hey Dolly. How's my girl?"

Dolly raised her head and looked at me. I rubbed her head and scratched her back. Usually she loved it, but on this occasion, she turned around and ignored me. Dolly could hold a grudge when she wanted to. Since she didn't want to be sociable, I looked under her blanket for her most recently collected treasures. I found two more rocks that I added to her growing pile. She had found the bowl end of a plastic spoon broken in half. She also had a bent Eisenhower dime, and a silver button, and all those items I took with me onto the bus and tossed them into the kitchen trash.

I thought for a moment about what I wanted to do to pass the time, then elected to write some music. There was a song I'd been working on for the better part of a week that was giving me some trouble. I had the lyrics where I wanted them, but there was something about the melody that I didn't like and wanted to change. The hard part was figuring out what that change was. Having the desire to figure it out, I went to my room, grabbed my notebook and my Martin, and took them back to the parlor. I got comfortable and strummed the guitar. I woke Merle up with the noise, but since he and the other animals were used to music on the bus, he put his head down again.

For several minutes, I worked through some chord progressions before changing the tune to a different key altogether. It turned out I hated that even worse, so I changed it back again, and worked through different iterations until I had something I was almost happy with. I picked up my pencil, made a few notations, and then, as was my habit, rather than put the pencil back on the table, I moved to place it between my lips. I lost fewer pencils when I chewed on them while I wrote. Just before the pencil touched my lips, I looked down and noticed a white substance against the yellow-painted wood. I brought the pencil closer to look at what it was, and then I saw the index finger and thumb of my right hand contained particles as well.

I moved over to the sink, turned on the water, rinsed my fingers, and watched as the substance combined with the water and disappeared down the sink.

Where had I seen that before?

I watched the water swirl in the bowl for a moment, then shut it off.

"Wait. Wait, a moment…"

I grabbed the kitchen trash bin, tipped it over, and then watched as the contents spread over the counter. Among the banana peels, a few crumpled sheets of paper, and a small amount of other random kitchen trash, I found what I was looking for. The button I had just thrown away. I picked it up and saw right away the white substance I had transferred to my fingers. I realized I had seen it before, and it took a simple swipe through the remaining refuse to find the flower stem I had thrown away the day before.

Certainly, I wasn't a chemist, but they looked the same to me, and at last the synapses in my brain connected enough to realize I'd seen it before. Literally right on the tip of my nose.

Flour.

From the bakery.

Somehow, Dolly had been exploring the area and brought back two items covered in flour. I studied the button and realized I had seen that before, too. I closed my eyes and mentally replayed conversations I'd had with anyone over the last few days. There was only one person I could remember who was wearing a jacket with buttons like this.

I smiled.

I had a new suspect.

CHAPTER THIRTEEN

My tunnel vision was in full effect when I stepped off the bus. I didn't notice Bozeman performing his post-run stretch, and tripped over his outstretched leg. My arms flailed before me, and I performed a graceful face plant in the dirt. To his credit, Bozeman didn't laugh, but he took a moment to help me up.

"Where are you going in such a hurry?" he asked.

I pointed across the lot. "To the bakery."

I left Bozeman behind and raced to the back door. Of course, I expected it to be locked, and it was. I pushed and pulled on the door but didn't get it to budge. I examined the area, and on the ground, a foot to the door's side, was a small pile of flour. Directly in the center of that pile looked to be a handprint, except it was too tiny to be a human hand, unless there was an infant loose in the parking lot. It was Dolly's. I tried the door again, and of course, it didn't move a single inch.

I looked up at the building and discovered a small window I hadn't noticed before. It was only about fourteen inches square, and even I wouldn't fit through it, but it would still give me an idea if anything was amiss inside. The problem was, I was about two feet too short to peer into it.

"Hey Bozeman, come over here. I need a boost."

To his credit, Bozeman didn't ask a single question. He simply came over and did what I needed him to do. I had him bend over. I put a foot in his cupped hands, and he lifted me easily over the ledge so I could gawk into the bakery. A fine dusting of flour covered the window. I tapped on the window, hoping some of the flour would drop away, and to my surprise, the window swung inward.

"Lift me a little higher, Boze."

Bozeman complied, and I grabbed the ledge and stuck my head through the open window. My shoulders were too wide for the opening, so I got no farther, but I was in enough to see the bakery's inside. For sure, someone had been there. There were a few pans and several other items on the floor. The usually clean stainless-steel counters and appliances all had a layer of white on them, like it had snowed inside the building. To me, it didn't seem like someone had vandalized it. More like someone had a tantrum and took it out on items within reach, like when people toss vases or lamps during outbursts in movies.

"Okay, you can let me down." I pulled the window closed as well as I could, and in a couple seconds my feet were back on the ground.

"What's going on?" Bozeman asked.

"Someone's been in there. It's a mess. The door's locked, and I suspect the front door is too. Sam says the only key is with the cops, so that means that either someone took it from them, or there's another key out there."

"So what?"

"Next to the sink on the bus are two items I took away from Dolly's stash. I guess one is the bottom part of a broken boutonniere, and the other is a button which I'm pretty sure came from a denim jacket."

"Where did Dolly get them?"

"Right around here. She left a footprint." I pointed to it, and

Bozeman squatted to inspect the area.

"Yeah, that's hers," he conceded.

"I encountered a denim jacket yesterday. Shanna was wearing it when she came to Sam's apartment with the note she found."

"You guess she's in on this?"

"Oh, yes, big time. Now I only need to find her."

"You realize that the phone you carry is good for more than phone calls and giving you directions. Where is it?"

"I left it on the bus."

A few moments later, Bozeman was looking through my phone while I gave Merle belly scratches. It took him only ten or fifteen minutes, but he soon picked up my pencil and jotted an address down in my notepad.

"She's over on Madison Street, about five blocks from here."

"How did you figure that out?"

Bozeman smiled and set my phone on the table. "I used the bakery's social media pages to find pictures of Shanna, which I used to do a similar image search until I found her personal pages. She doesn't have them set to private, and in one photo she had a photo of a birthday card she received, but she didn't block out or hide the address. Not very smart. Anyone can find her."

I leaned over and gave him a hug. "Thanks, Boze. I'm so glad you're smarter than you appear."

Bozeman grinned. "I know. That isn't too hard. Are you going out again? Do you need me to go with you?"

"No. I'll take Betty, and I'll be okay."

"Alright then. I'm jumping in the shower. Take your phone with you and call me if you get into any trouble, which, knowing you, is a distinct possibility."

I tore the sheet from the pad, left the table, strapped Betty in for the journey, and jumped from the bus. I knew where Jefferson Street was, so I assumed they were in presidential order and figured Madison had to be the next block over. To my surprise, I was right. I was getting better at this navigation stuff.

Shanna's house was in the middle of the block, a quaint-looking Craftsman style home with a few potted flowers on the front porch. I was undecided whether I wanted to go in aggressive with guns blazing, or passive like I was just passing through. Shanna decided for me when the door opened before I'd even reached for the doorbell.

"What are you doing here?" she asked.

"Just figured I'd stop by and check on how you're doing and if you've talked to Sam."

Shanna let go of the door and moved into the living room. Although she hadn't invited me in, I followed her anyway and took a seat on her couch. She paced across the room and back before she settled into a wooden rocking chair near the front window.

"No. She's in jail. How would I have talked to her?"

I looked around for the jacket she wore yesterday, but it wasn't in the room. I doubted she'd let me search the rest of the house for it.

"Do you wonder what you're going to do next? Like if Sam goes to prison and can't run the bakery?"

Shanna smiled. "I'm going to run it. Keep the bakery going."

That was a surprise to me. Sam had mentioned Shanna wasn't ready for the big time yet.

"You've talked about that with her?" I asked.

Shanna hesitated. "Oh, sure. We've talked about it. Like, not in the context of her going to jail, but like what if she got really sick, or wanted to take an extended vacation? Scenarios like that."

Somehow, I doubted that's how the conversation actually happened. Besides, she looked up and to the left, so I suspected she was lying. Or was it up and to the right? I never remembered which way it was. Didn't matter. I still had her dead to rights.

"The bakery wasn't open today, was it? I could really go for one of those muffins. You haven't been over there, have you?"

"No. Like I said, I haven't talked to Sam yet, but I'm sure

she'll want me to get it back in business as soon as I can."

"You haven't been over there?" I asked again.

"I said no. Not since…Saturday. Yeah, it was Saturday morning."

"Oh yes, I remember now. When that awful man came in."

Anger flushed through Shanna's face so quickly I almost mistook it for a lapse in my vision. She looked at her feet, then at the ceiling, then at the wall behind me.

"What did you think of Sherman?" I asked.

Her eyes continued to flit around the room, and finally they settled on me.

"He was… I never had… I don't know," Shanna sputtered.

"Why not? No one else I talked to liked him. He seemed to be a mean, spiteful man, only in search of his next dollar."

Shanna smiled. "Oh, no. He had his sweet side too, he…"

Somewhere in another room, I heard a phone ring. Shanna excused herself and left to answer the call.

While she was gone, I sat still and looked around. It was a modest living room. Besides the couch and the rocking chair, there was a small side table next to the couch, holding a lamp. There was a basket overflowing with magazines next to the rocking chair, and a wooden teacart on which a small television sat. On the wall behind the television, I saw framed family photos, so I got up and studied the pictures. The one that caught my attention was a photo where a lawman was standing with two small kids on either side. A boy and a girl.

"That's my dad with me and my brother."

I hadn't heard Shanna approach, so she startled me, not that I wanted to give her that satisfaction. "Your dad was a cop?"

"Yep. Spent thirty years with the New Mexico State Patrol. Retired a few years ago and moved to Florida."

"Why Florida?"

Shanna shrugged. "No clue. He never really gave us a good reason for that, just said all retired people should move to Florida."

I leaned a little closer to the photo, and I could just make out his name tag. J. Jennings. Holy moly. Jennings. "Um, your brother wouldn't be Chief Jennings, would he?"

"Yes. Daddy was so proud that one of us followed in his footsteps. He practically burst his buttons when Jack made chief."

I figured right then I had a problem with her brother being the chief. It was a struggle, but I smiled anyway. "I'll bet he did. Speaking of buttons, did you lose one lately?" I played it cool and returned to the couch.

"I'm not sure what you mean."

"On that jacket you came to Sam's in. The denim jacket. It has those distinctive buttons. I found one today, covered in flour, and I'll bet if we looked at that jacket, we'd find you're missing a button."

"So what? Lots of people lose buttons."

"Yeah, but you told me you haven't been to the bakery in a couple days. Obviously, that was a lie."

I expected her to confess to her crimes a la every dramatic courtroom scene I've ever seen on television, but Shanna just stared at me, not speaking, not moving.

I stepped in with both barrels. "Shanna, I think you did it. You killed Sherman Stier, and you killed Hanson when he saw you do it. Then you let Sam take the blame. I just don't understand why you'd do it."

A flashing light caught my eye. I looked out the window and saw the chief getting out of his car. I smiled. "The calvary has arrived."

Shanna grinned even wider as she reached to open the door. "It's not what you expect."

Chief Jennings entered the room and nodded at Shanna, then approached me. "Get up and turn around."

I didn't understand. "What? Wait!"

The chief didn't wait. Instead, he grabbed me by the upper arm and lifted me with ease to my feet. He spun me around, and before I realized what happened, He handcuffed me and marched me right out of the house.

"What is this?" I yelled as he forced me down the sidewalk. "She's the one. She did it."

"You're under arrest for trespassing." He bent me over the hood of the car. I saw neighbors coming out of their houses to watch the show. That was going to be great for my public image. I considered for the briefest of moments making my booking photo the cover art for my next album.

"What's this?" The chief found Betty, removed her from my holster, removed the clip, checked the chamber, and set the gun on the hood. "I guess I need to add carrying a concealed weapon to the charges."

"I've got a permit for that. It's in my wallet."

Jennings ignored me as he checked my other pockets for weapons. He didn't find guns or knives, but he found my phone and wallet. After he was done, he placed me in the backseat of his squad and got in the front.

He turned in his seat so he could face me. "You want to explain what you're doing here?"

I didn't know if I wanted to. He was her brother. How could I accuse her of a double murder to her brother? I wouldn't think that would have the impact I wanted. I needed to see how far I could stretch the truth without throwing out any accusations.

"Sheriff, I only came over to talk to her. About if she's seen Sam, and about the bakery."

"Why?"

"I told you before, Sam's my friend."

"Sure, fine. But why would you care about the bakery? You don't live here. You don't have a vested interest in it."

Okay, he had me there. I shrugged my shoulders. "I like the blueberry muffins she makes. Come on, chief, let me go. I just came over here to talk. Nothing more."

"Shanna said you forced your way in uninvited and wouldn't leave. Are you saying that's not true?"

"No. Look, I don't expect you to trust me. I have proof back at my bus."

"What proof?"

"Dolly found a button from Shanna's jacket, and one of Hanson's flowers."

"So, you want me to get a statement from Dolly?"

"No. You can't talk to her. Dolly's a raccoon." I knew I made a mistake the second the rushed words passed my lips.

"Raccoon? You collected evidence from a raccoon? Did the raccoon give you a statement? Does it talk? Can it give a description to my department sketch artist?"

At that moment, I wished I could put my hands over my face and hide.

"Have you had any drugs or alcohol today?"

I shook my head. "No, I don't do those. I'm sober."

He didn't take that as gospel either. Based on the Dolly talk, I couldn't blame him.

"Perhaps I should talk to another officer. Do you have someone else I could talk to? Like maybe Deputy Samuels?"

He rolled his eyes. "You obviously don't know how that works. Complaints go up the chain of command, not down, and I'm at the top of the chain. Why would you need someone else? Are you going to lodge a protest?"

I was getting frustrated. "No. That's your sister in there. Surely, you're going to take her side about anything I have to say."

"You assume I can't be impartial?"

I shrugged and noticed the insulted look on his face. I struggled a bit, but I managed to sit up straighter. "No."

"You're wrong. If it's one thing my daddy instilled in me was a love for the law, and he also taught me that the law was equal for all people."

I swallowed. Maybe I had more in common with him than I thought. "My dad told me the same thing. Nothing made him angrier than when rich people got to skirt around the law while some lawmen harassed the poor."

That got his attention. "Your father was a cop?"

I nodded. "Detective with the Denver police."

His voice softened. "You see it all the time. Lots of criminals think they can get away with stealing the moon because they have relatives who wear a badge. Makes me sick. I'm not like that. If I caught Shanna driving drunk through town, or high on drugs, or running naked down Main Street, or holding up the pharmacy at gunpoint, you can bet your bottom dollar that I'd have no second thoughts about arresting her."

"Why all the aggression with me? I did nothing wrong. I came here to talk, not shoot her to death."

"Then why are you carrying a gun?"

"After the event Saturday night, I walked alone back to the lot behind the bakery where we parked the bus. I thought someone was following me," I said.

I wasn't sure if he believed me or not.

"Who was it?" Sheriff Jennings asked.

"I don't know. All I heard were the footsteps, and when I looked behind me, I didn't spot anyone. It freaked me out."

"Can anyone confirm that?"

I thought for a second. "Yeah. I ran into the ice cream place on Main Street. I told the guy there."

"Bigger guy? Gray hair and mustache?"

"That's him."

"Paul Patterson. What did Paul do? Call the police?"

"No. He looked around outside, but there was no one there by that point. He offered to walk me back to the bus, but I declined. After that, I started carrying the gun for my protection. Like I said, it's registered and I have a permit."

Chief Jennings opened my wallet and found the paper. He scrutinized it for a few moments, then put it back where he found it.

"This is all a big misunderstanding," I said. "Why don't we go back in there and talk to Shanna and straighten everything out? Or we could go back to my bus and I'll show you what I found."

"Okay. You wait here. Don't move."

Chief Jennings left the car and returned to the house. From where I sat, I saw him knock on the door, then enter.

"Don't move. Funny," I said aloud to no one. I couldn't if I wanted to since I wore the handcuffs. Even if I got out of those, I'm sure he locked the back doors. And there was a plastic partition preventing me from going into the front seat, and I surely could not dig my way through the backseat into the trunk. I waited patiently for the chief to return.

I expected him to return right away, but he didn't. After five or six minutes, I wondered what kind of fairy tales Shanna was telling about me.

At last, the door opened, and Chief Jennings came out. He was moving fast, but not quite running. He seemed to know that the neighbors were still watching. Rather than get back in the car, he came to my side and opened the door.

"Get out."

I did as I was told, and he turned me around and gently removed the cuffs. He opened the passenger door. "Get in."

I got in the front seat and waited for him to slide into the driver's seat. "Are we going to talk to Shanna?"

He picked up the radio handset. "No. She's gone. He pressed the button. Unit one to base."

The radio crackled for a second, then the response came through. "Go ahead, Chief."

"Base, I need you to put a BOLO out on Shanna Prescott. She's probably driving a silver Ford pickup. If anyone spots her, don't approach. Just let me know where she is."

"Copy that, Chief."

"Unit one out." Jennings replaced the handset and started the engine.

"Now what?" I asked.

"Now we're going to your bus. I want to see what you

have."

The chief did a U-turn in the street and headed for the bakery. It didn't take over three minutes to drive the short distance, and he parked the patrol car and followed me into the bus.

Bozeman was watching TV when he saw the chief appear. He got to his feet immediately, let me pass, then stepped into the space to separate me from the chief. "What's going on here, Codi? Everything okay?"

"Everything's fine, Bozeman. He just wants to see what Dolly found." I glanced around for a moment. The items were still on the counter. "Where's Merle?"

"Downstairs with Dolly."

"Who's Merle?" the chief asked.

"He's… my cat." I almost lost him trying to explain Dolly. I didn't want to have to explain why I also hung out with a skunk. "Over here."

I pointed to the items on the counter and stepped aside to give him room to look. Rather than touch them, he bent over to get a closer look.

"What do you think?"

He stood straight again. "Yeah, that looks like a button from her jacket. It's her favorite, so I've seen her in it probably a thousand times. I don't get the significance of the twig, though."

"I didn't either until I went to the florist's shop to see Hanson. That green tape at the bottom is a florist's tape that they used to hold flowers and such together. I'm pretty sure that's the remains of the boutonniere Hanson wore on Saturday night. I'm also certain the white substance on both items is flour."

"You have a couple of plastic bags?"

Bozeman was closest to the pantry, so he opened the door and handed a couple of baggies to the chief. Chief Jennings took a steak knife from the butcher block and used the knife to push the items over the counter's edge and into their respective baggies. He put the knife back, sealed the bags, and stuffed them both into his shirt pocket.

"What makes you think it's flour?"

"Come on, I'll show you."

I led Jennings out into the parking lot, and over to the bakery. There, I pointed out Dolly's tiny footprint. He took a few pictures with his phone, then collected a sample of the white powder into another baggie. Since he was taller than me, he had no trouble boosting himself up to the window like I had done and taking a peek inside. After he took a couple more pictures, he led me back to the cruiser and gave back my belongings, including my gun, which I returned directly to its holster.

"Well, chief, what do you think?" Bozeman asked.

The chief looked at Bozeman and pointed a thumb in my direction. "I think that Codi's on to something here, as baffling as it sounds."

"It was the raccoon that convinced you, wasn't it?" I asked.

The Chief was about to answer when the radio unit he carried squawked. "Base to unit one."

"Go ahead."

"Chief, someone spotted Prescott's car speeding west out of town. As requested, the deputy held back, but followed at a distance. Prescott went up to the construction site. Do you have further orders?"

"Have the deputy stay there, but don't pursue. I'm on the way. I'm out."

He looked at me as he opened the door. "Well? Are you coming?"

CHAPTER FOURTEEN

I didn't need to be asked twice, so I jumped in the car and by the time I reached for my seatbelt, we were already speeding out of the lot. As Chief Jenning drove, I kept my mouth shut and watched the outside world pass by faster than I had ever before. Jennings slowed at intersections to ensure we'd get through safely, but only slightly. I sat in awe as we ran through red lights and as cars pulled over to let us pass. I took the ride as a proxy power trip.

Once we got outside of town, Jennings stomped the accelerator like he was executing a cockroach, and we shot through the scrubland like a rocket ship. I glimpsed another patrol car ahead and thought for sure Jennings wouldn't be able to stop in time. But I admit, it impressed me when we came to a halt within a foot of the other car without so much as a squeal from the brakes.

The deputy came alongside, and Jennings rolled down his window. "She still up there?"

The deputy turned and looked up at the road and back at the chief. I noticed the deputy was a woman, tall, skinny. Her uniform shirt looked too large for her, and it billowed in the breeze like a ship's sail.

"Yes, sir. Unless she drove off the road on the far side of the property, but I think there are still old cattle fences out that way, aren't there?"

"I think so. Stay here in case she doubles back. I'm going up to find her. If you don't hear from me in fifteen minutes, call dispatch for some backup."

"Okay, Chief."

The deputy backed away and watched us pass, and the chief turned onto a gravel road. Unlike before, when he drove fast enough to peel the paint from the car, this time he barely crept along.

"Does this road lead to the new resort?" I asked.

"Yeah."

"I thought it wasn't under construction yet."

"Most of it isn't. The first phase is laying sewer and prepping the land for the building foundations," the sheriff said as he steered around a pothole. "That's where they are now."

"Why would Shanna come up here?"

He didn't answer. The only sounds came from the crunch of the gravel beneath the tires and the occasional chirp from the radio. We got to the top of a rise, and below I discovered where they laid out the bare bones of the resort. I saw stacks of unlaid sewer line, several trenches dug, and large machines lined up along the road. There were lots of stakes sticking out of the ground with pink ribbons waving in the breeze. Throughout the property, roads of gravel resembling tendrils spread out in several directions.

At the far end of the area, I spotted a construction trailer with the contractor's name on the side, and two other sheds. As we drove closer and rounded a bend, I caught sight of Shanna's truck parked behind a shed. I didn't spot her, only the open door of her Ford. Jennings slowed the vehicle and pressed on until he parked on the opposite side of the shed from the truck.

"Stay here," he ordered. The stare he gave me matched his

stern words.

He opened the door, stepped outside, and I watched as he used the shed's corner for cover, determined it was clear and slipped around to its side. Not wanting to miss anything, I disobeyed orders and followed his trail. I met up with him soon after, and when he discovered me coming, he put a hand up for me to stop and shook his head. He put a finger to his lips, so I tried to be quiet.

Jennings crouched behind Shanna's truck. With his gun drawn and with a quick motion, he popped up, looked into the truck's bed and got down when he realized it stood empty. Slowly, he made his way to the open door, peered in, and came back to me.

"She's armed," he whispered.

"How do you know?"

"The rifle rack is empty, so she must have it on her. You should get back in the car and drive back to the deputy. I made a mistake bringing you down here."

"Well, I'm not going back. You should either arrest me, or let's press on." It was a tossup to which one he'd choose, but in the end, he nodded.

"At least stay behind me or something else. Stay out of the line of fire. I'm going into the construction trailer next. You stay outside. I mean it this time."

We edged to the end of the shed, and I got a good view of the trailer. It looked like a manufactured home, but it stood on wheels and had cinderblocks beneath it to keep it level and steady. We were on the end of the trailer, which contained an air conditioner unit and no windows, so we made quick time hustling up against the building.

Jennings took a snap look around the corner. "There's only one door in, and three small windows. I didn't see any rifle barrels sticking out, so that's a good sign. You stay here. I'm going in. Okay?"

I nodded, and Jennings crept around the corner. True to my

word, I stayed put. Well, I kind of stayed put. I tiptoed to the corner and looked around it. Jennings stood still by the door with his hand on the knob. He opened the door an inch while I held my breath.

"Shanna? It's me, it's Jack. I want to come in there and talk to you, okay?"

"No." Shanna screamed loud enough that I easily understood her.

Jennings opened the door wider so he could peek in. I worried he was making another mistake, especially if she really had a rifle.

"Shanna come on, put the gun down, and I'll come in and we can talk about it, okay? Everything's going to be fine. Look, I'm going to put my gun away, and you can put yours away, okay?"

If Shanna answered, I didn't pick it up. She must have relented, though, because Chief Jennings holstered his sidearm and moved inside, leaving the door open.

I moved around the corner, so I had a better chance of eavesdropping.

"Shanna, put the rifle down. Daddy told you never to point a gun at a person, remember? Remember, he taught us both that? Do you remember how important that was to him? To never point a gun at someone? Put it down, Shanna."

Shanna murmured something in response.

"Tell me, why did you run from the house? Why did you tell me Codi broke in on you? What's going on? Talk to me Shanna."

Again, I got no response.

"Shanna, NO!"

Chief Jennings screamed the last word, and I caught the rifle's report. It hadn't even finished ringing in my ears, and I was already trying to figure out what to do. Go back for the deputy? Run in like the savior? I seemed trapped between opposite reactions, but I decided quickly when I realized the chief might need immediate help, and I couldn't leave him.

I reached around and pulled Betty from my holster and held her down by my side. When I moved, I positioned myself right in front of the door. Once there, I glanced inside where one of Chief Jennings' legs stretched out in front of me, unmoving.

"Shanna? This is Codi Cassidy. I'm coming in now. I don't mean you harm. Let me check on the chief, okay?"

I got no words, but a loud wail that transformed into a heavy sob. I stuck in my head far enough to peek and looked toward Shanna. She sat on top of a desk, her hands in front of her face, crying. The rifle stood on the floor in front of her. I kicked it into gear, rushed into the room, grabbed it by the still-warm barrel, and chucked it out of the trailer.

"I, I, I k-k-killed my only brother." Shanna sobbed and bawled even harder.

I didn't want to look, but I did. Chief Jennings laid face down in front of a filing cabinet. I thought he was dead, but I noticed his body shake, and he stirred slightly.

"Help me," he sputtered.

I honored his soft plea and helped him roll onto his back. Shanna hadn't killed him after all. The shot got him in the shoulder, and the impact spun him around and he fell, hitting his head against the file cabinet on his way down.

"Shanna. You didn't kill him. He's not dead. He's moving."

Shanna was still crying, but she dropped her hands and looked over at us. Chief Jennings threw her a half-hearted wave.

Without prompting, Shanna rambled. "I didn't mean to do it. I just got so angry with him. He said he loved me. He said he'd take me away from here once the resort was done. But when he came to the bakery that morning, and didn't even acknowledge me, I knew it was all a lie. I was just another toy to him."

I helped the chief sit up, and he leaned his back against the cabinet. "Shanna, what did you do?"

"It was an accident. I had a knife from the bakery, and I was… practicing with it at home. I didn't think Sam would even miss it, but then I felt guilty, and I was going to return it to her that night. There I was in the kitchen when Sam came bursting through the door and then Sherman came in after her. I took him into the pantry and I told him I loved him and that he should forget about the stupid bakery. But he said he didn't love me. He wanted the bakery. He wanted her. Don't you understand?"

Jennings and I looked at each other, then back at her.

Shanna sniffed, then wiped her nose on the sleeve of her denim jacket, and I noticed right then, that yes, the bottom button was gone.

No one said a word, but it was Shanna who lost the game of silence first. "When he tried to push his way past me, I got him. He fell, and I left the pantry and ran back to the kitchen. I was going nutty in there and didn't know what to do, so I went back to the pantry, and that's when I saw HER on the floor next to HIM, and I lost it. I refused to take it. She didn't deserve him, only I did. I screamed, and when the others came, I went back to the kitchen."

"Why did you stick around?" Jennings asked.

Shanna shrugged. "I wanted to see if he was still alive, and when I found out he wasn't, the police were already there and wouldn't let me leave. And then what did I see? I saw her talking to you!"

Shanna punctuated her sentence by pointing at me. I was glad I had the foresight to toss the rifle outside.

"The next thing I knew, you were waltzing around the room like the queen, asking stupid questions, and I knew you had to be dealt with, too. After you finished talking with me, I returned to the kitchen to find myself another knife, but I didn't. The best I got was one of Sam's pie cutters. I was so furious I couldn't wait to get you outside."

Shanna laughed to herself. "Do you get how happy it made me when you walked back to the bakery instead of riding in that big bus of yours? I was ecstatic."

"It was you who followed me."

Shanna nodded. "I almost got you, too, but then you turned that corner, and those kids were across the street. I knew I lost my chance when you ran into the ice cream parlor."

For once, my intuition was on point.

"After that, every time I tried to find you, you weren't alone. Lucky for you."

I looked at Jennings. He didn't look good. Nearby was a work shirt draped over a chair. It looked clean enough. I balled it up and applied pressure to his shoulder. His head was bleeding too, but I didn't have another compress, and his shoulder was much worse. He gritted his teeth but otherwise took the pain without complaint.

"What about Hanson Johns? How did he fit in?" Jennings asked.

"Sunday morning, out of the blue, he called me and said he saw me there. He wanted me to give him five thousand dollars, or he was going to turn me over to you. Yeah. Like I have five thousand dollars just lying around. If I did, I wouldn't have come back to Quincey, that's for sure. We agreed to meet at the flower shop at one, and when we met, I lured him into that cooler and gave him the present I had meant for her."

Again, she pointed at me. I got the feeling we wouldn't be best friends.

"Then I thought, why don't I get rid of her first, so I could get to you next, even though I had planned it the other way around? That was the easiest thing ever. I just made that fake note and got you to believe I was being threatened, and when I turned it over to Jacky here, he couldn't arrest Sam fast enough. Good riddance. She deserved it for taking my man away, although I'd rather see her go to the cemetery than to prison."

I was so concerned about Jennings' shoulder that I had paid little attention to Shanna, other than passing glances. I looked over at her and saw she'd transformed. When I first entered the trailer, she was upset, almost hysterical about shooting the chief. Now she was sitting there calmly, relaying this story to us like we were chatting while having tea. Her tears had dried up, and although her eyes were red and puffy, they now had an appearance that leaned toward evil rather than sadness. She looked psychotic.

I leaned over and whispered into the chief's ear. "Where are your handcuffs?"

"Left side." His voice was weak. His shoulder wound didn't appear fatal, so I guessed he'd suffered a concussion when he hit his head. I reached over his body and got his cuffs.

"Chief? Stay awake. Don't go to sleep." I yelled his name and shook him gently. His left eye opened and tried to focus on me but he couldn't. "Shanna, your brother needs an ambulance. Can you call for help? There's a deputy just up the road."

"No. In fact, I've come up with a brand-new and improved plan. A much better one. I've decided you're going to prison with Sam."

"For what? I did nothing wrong."

"For killing the chief of police. You'll probably get the chair for that."

I looked up and noticed that Shanna had Betty pointed in my direction. How in the world did I lose my gun? Then I remembered. I set Betty on the table when I grabbed the shirt. Dumb. I wouldn't make that mistake again. Even if I lived through this.

"Although I have a better idea. I'll explain you shot Chief Jennings when he confronted you about killing the others, then I shot you. It's a winner-winner chicken dinner scenario for me. I'll probably be a hero. I'll have my picture in the paper and everything. Maybe Mayor Idiot will even give me a key to this stupid city."

That story made no sense to me. Why would I shoot anyone? I have no motive since I've only known these people for three days.

I detected a faint siren in the distance. Finally, the posse was on the way.

"Hey, Shanna? The police are almost here. Drop my gun and step back. You're finished."

Shanna moved back and glanced out the window. "You're right, time is running out. Say goodbye to the chief." Shanna pulled the trigger.

In the tiny trailer, the sound was deafening, even though Betty was only a .22. As expected, the muzzle flashed when the gun erupted, but no bullet came whizzing by. Only the shell casing that did a lazy loop in the air and bounced off the wall and onto the floor.

It was my turn to grin. "You can't kill him with blanks." I got up and took a step toward her. "Give it up. You can't hurt us anymore. Give me my gun back."

It was a bluff. Only the first bullet in the clip was a blank, but she didn't know that. I hoped she would drop the gun and give up. She didn't. Instead, she pulled the trigger again, and this time I felt the bullet rush past my head and the chief yelped like a kicked dog behind me. There was a pair of scissors and a large stapler on the table next to me, so I grabbed the stapler and threw it with all my might in her direction. My plan involved causing enough distraction so I could run out of the open door to safety.

Shanna fired again when I made my move. She was the best shot in the world, or I was the luckiest person on the planet because the bullet clipped the stapler enough to change its direction slightly. Rather than take a round to the chest, I got hit in the shoulder. I didn't have another chance to do anything else. Behind Shanna, a window broke, and then the world lit up.

I was only vaguely aware of the flurry of activity around me. I felt the trailer rock as several people entered, and I heard people screaming, although I couldn't understand the words. As my vision came back, I saw Deputy Samuels had Shanna in custody and was escorting her from the building. I sensed someone nearby, and the deputy I had met only a few minutes earlier was at my side, helping me to my feet. With her help, I staggered outside and collapsed on the ground when I got a few feet from the door.

An ambulance arrived, and the paramedics rushed into the building to tend to Jennings, and I tried to get up, but I couldn't.

"Whoa, there, tough girl." The deputy held me down, and I blinked a few times and hoped my mind would clear enough to read her tag. She noticed my struggle. "Can you hear me?"

I nodded.

"You can call me Daisy. We threw in a flash-bang grenade when we heard the gunshots. You'll be okay. You have some ringing in your ears?"

Ringing was an understatement. I nodded again.

"Don't worry. That will go away in a few minutes. Your normal vision will return too. Are you injured?"

"I got a bullet to the shoulder," I said.

"You don't have to yell. Just use your normal speaking voice." Daisy gave me a bottle of water, and I struggled to swallow the first mouthful. The fresh liquid helped clear my mind and my throat from the smoke created by the grenade. As I drank, Daisy tore my shirt and looked at my shoulder.

"You're not bleeding, but you'll probably have a hell of a bruise. Are you sure she shot you?"

I nodded for the third time. "Yes. It was a rubber bullet, though, and it hit something before it hit me, so I was doubly lucky. Is the chief going to be okay?"

"I don't know. They're working on him now."

Daisy stayed with me, and together we watched the trailer's door. After an eternity passed, two men carried the chief out through the narrow door, then put him on a gurney, and put the gurney on the ambulance. A few seconds later, the ambulance left, sirens blaring, leaving only a cloud of dust behind.

Deputy Samuels appeared and crouched down before me. "Chief Jennings will be fine, I think. He has a shoulder wound and a concussion for sure, and a possible broken rib or two. We'll have to wait for the x-rays to see for sure. Are you okay?"

"I think so," I said.

"Good. Deputy Daisy will take you to the hospital to get that shoulder checked out."

I was going to argue that it was fine, but it started to throb and stiffen. "Okay."

Daisy and Samuels helped me to my feet and into Daisy's car. As Daisy got in the driver's seat, Samuels buckled me in.

He gave me a smile. "It'll all be okay. Oh, and don't leave town. I'll have some questions for you."

I looked him in the eyes. As I focused, I noticed he had pretty green eyes, with a speck of gold in the bottom of one iris. "I should have left town three days ago."

Samuels nodded and closed the door. I rested my head against the window and closed my eyes. A few moments later, we were on the move.

CHAPTER FIFTEEN

The next day I slept in. Normally I was an early riser, but I was dead tired, which, in retrospect, was better than being just dead. I opened my eyes around eleven in the morning and I woke to a pair of pretty kitty eyes staring at me.

"Hey Gibson. Are you trying to steal my soul?" I got an arm above the covers and scratched his ears. Gibson purred in response, then jumped off the bed and ran from the room.

I got up, did my morning business, then returned to my room. Rather than the full cowgirl regalia, I slipped into a pair of teal sweatpants. Before I pulled on my T-shirt, I studied my shoulder in the mirror. The x-rays confirmed I had no broken bones the day before. The rubber bullet didn't break the skin, but a large, deep red bruise the size of a half dollar had already developed. It hurt to look at it, so I didn't bother trying to touch it.

I ran a brush through my hair, and brushed my teeth, and, feeling somewhat normal, I ventured out into the world.

The bus was empty, so I assumed Bozeman was outside, and when I stepped down the stairs, I found him waiting for me.

"Sleep well?" Bozeman asked as he put the magazine he was holding down in his lap.

"I did. It must have been the painkillers they gave me at the hospital."

"Hungry? I could make you some eggs," he said.

Bozeman reminded me of my mother that way. They both carried the superstition that food would cure any ailment, hurt feelings, unpleasant experiences, or any general malaise.

"Not really. I could go for one of those, though." I pointed to the bucket of small orange juice bottles Bozeman had near his chair. He passed me a bottle. I opened it and drank. It tasted delicious.

"How's your shoulder? Is it going to be okay?"

I knew Bozeman was concerned, but I also guessed he was hinting around to see if I could play our next gig on Saturday night, which, by my count, was only three days away.

"It should be. I've got a nasty bruise, and it's a little stiff, but I should be ready to go."

"If you're not up to it, we could get a session player to stand in for you. I have a few guitarists in mind who could fill in."

That was the beauty of being me. Although I considered myself a talented songwriter, and of course, a great singer, Bozeman was the lead guitarist, and I mostly only played the rhythm. We could hire just about anyone to do that. Especially for the more traditional country songs we typically had on our set list. Those were usually simple three or four chord progression numbers with not much complication. And many of them were well-known country standards that any guitarist worth their weight already knew.

"Let's see how I feel tomorrow. I should be able to know for sure if I can play," I said.

Bozeman picked up his magazine and found the page he was on. "Fair enough."

I took another drink of orange juice, then looked at the sky. It had the makings of another beautiful day. The sun was bright;

the sky was a light blue, and I tracked but a single cloud as it raced across the troposphere. I closed my eyes and felt the sun's warmth on my face.

"You have a visitor coming," Bozeman announced.

I opened my eyes and turned my head, and saw Sam walking across the parking lot carrying something covered by a towel. When she got to us, she handed the item to Bozeman.

"Hey there," she said to me.

"Hey yourself." I got to my feet, and we hugged. My shoulder was tender and throbbed during the embrace, but I still didn't want to let go, and apparently Sam didn't want to let go either. Finally, we separated.

"I was over earlier, but Bozeman told me you were still sleeping."

I turned to Bozeman. "You didn't tell me she was here."

He shrugged. "I forgot."

"I assumed you might be hungry." Sam lifted the towel and exposed the four blueberry muffins on a plate.

My mouth watered like one of Pavlov's dogs, and I reached for one.

"You told me you weren't hungry," Bozeman said as he pulled the plate away.

"That was before. This is now."

Bozeman brought the plate forward, and I took the muffin. I held it beneath my nose and inhaled. Oh, that smell!

"Here, Sam, take my seat." Bozeman set the plate on a bus step and selected a muffin for himself. "I'll go see what the kids are up to."

Sam grabbed a muffin from the plate and handed it to Bozeman. "Here, they can have one too. There are plenty more where these came from."

Bozeman took the muffin and sauntered off to give the animals a treat.

Sam and I hugged again, and then we both sat.

"When did you get out of the pokey?" I asked.

"Last night around ten. I was just in there reading a book, and the next thing I knew the cell door opened, and in walked Shanna in an orange jumpsuit. They brought her in and took me out."

"I would've loved to see the look on your face."

"Me too. Come on. Shanna? I never would have guessed it was her."

With great anticipation, I peeled the paper from the muffin's bottom and broke off a chunk. I liked to eat the bottom first and save the crown for last. I was weird that way.

"Me either."

"Is it true she tried to kill you?" Sam asked.

I nodded as I popped a piece into my mouth and chewed. My eyes rolled as I savored the bite and then swallowed. "Yes. She probably would have too if I used real ammunition. She hurt Chief Jennings really badly though. Have you heard how he's doing?"

"No."

"Did you know they are siblings?" I asked.

"No. Neither one ever mentioned it to me. I can't imagine why."

I shrugged, ate another part of the muffin, and drank some juice.

"Listen, I had to come over and thank you for everything you've done for me. I wouldn't be free if it wasn't for you," Sam said. She didn't have to say a word. Her expression told me all I needed.

I smiled. "Anytime."

We sat for a moment in silence, staring at each other.

Sam leaned forward. "You didn't mean that, did you?"

I laughed. "Actually, no. I don't enjoy getting shot."

Sam smiled. "I don't blame you." Sam stood. "Listen, I need to go. The bakery's still a mess, and I need to get that cleaned up. And I have a million orders to fill."

"You need any help?" I asked.

"From you, no. One other thing, Lisa's having a small get together later at the diner. Starts at seven. Make sure you and that hunk are there, okay?"

"We'll be there."

I sat back in the chair and finished my muffin and looked forward to a lazy day.

At seven on the dot, Bozeman and I walked through the diner's door. They had rearranged the room a bit, and pushed several tables together in the center of the room to form one big seating area. Around the table were most of the people I'd interacted with over the previous days. Sam, Dean, Reba, and Pastor Tom were all in attendance. As we approached and said our hellos, Rob and Lisa appeared from the kitchen carrying dishes of food they placed on the table to serve family style. Bozeman and I found our seats, and Pastor Tom started the meal off with a quick prayer.

When the blessing was over, I looked around the table at the food. There was a platter holding a mountain of fried chicken. There were big bowls filled with mashed potatoes, buttered corn, and green beans with slivered almonds. Of course, there was not one, but two baskets of fresh-baked dinner rolls.

A server appeared and took our drink orders. Bozeman asked for a beer. I asked for lemonade. Soon, plates we passed around the table and filled them, and the sound of small talk and clinking silverware filled the air.

Everyone stopped eating and looked up when the door opened, and Deputy Samuels entered.

Rob stood and held out his hand for Samuels to shake. "Deputy, please, join us. There's plenty of food."

Samuels shook his head. "Unfortunately, I can't. I'm on duty. I'm in charge while Chief Jennings takes some time to mend."

"How's he doing?" I asked,

"He's good. The worst he got was the concussion, so they're keeping him under observation for another day or two for that.

Otherwise, they patched up the shoulder pretty good."

"What about his ribs? Broken?"

Samuels shook his head. "No. Only bruised. Good thing you had non-lethal rounds in that gun. Oh, that reminds me, the chief wanted me to give this to you." Samuels reached into his coat and handed me an evidence bag. Betty was inside.

"I didn't expect I'd ever see this again. I assumed you'd need it for the trial."

"It's unnecessary. We've already got Shanna on two counts of murder. The chief's not bothering with the added assault charge. He also asked me to give you a message. Asked me to write it down even so I wouldn't get it wrong."

We all waited while Samuels extracted a piece of paper from his shirt pocket. He unfolded it, cleared his throat, and read directly from the paper. "Codi, please accept my gratitude. I'm in your debt. If I could ask you for one more favor, please leave my town as soon as you can."

I protested. "That's not what it says!"

Samuels handed me the paper, and I read it. He had read it word for word from the sheet.

"Son of a gun," I said.

Everyone at the table laughed at the joke at my expense, including Bozeman.

"By the way, the chief also wanted me to tell you that he turned all the evidence you had against Shanna to me, since I'll be doing the investigation. He didn't want anyone to expect he couldn't be impartial since his sister is the accused."

I smiled. "Thank him for me. That means a lot."

A squawk came from Samuels' radio. He answered the call, excused himself, and rushed from the room.

The meal continued on, and as the servers cleared the table from dinner, Dean stood and clinked a fork against his glass to get our attention.

"Hey, everyone. I just wanted to make a toast to Sam and welcome her back." He waited as the rest of us applauded but didn't take his seat. He looked uncomfortable, but he spoke again. "I'd also like to apologize to everyone here. I've been going through some… things, and it's been a personal struggle for me. Because of that, I haven't been on my best behavior, and I've been a rotten friend to all of you. I'm sorry. Sam, I've been especially hard on you, and I would accept being your friend, even if you never want nothing more than that."

Sam smiled, then stood and gave Dean a hug. "We'll always be friends, Dean. All of us here will always be friends."

Rob interrupted. "Not friends, family."

Everyone applauded again as Dean and Sam sat.

I leaned over to Bozeman. "I wonder what's for dessert."

Lisa overheard my question. "We'll serve dessert shortly. Give it a little time. Let your dinner settle."

I looked across the table at Reba. She winked at me, then produced a bottle of white wine, filled her water glass, and an instant later, the bottle disappeared again. She was quite the magician, and amazingly, I don't think anyone else at the table noticed, and if they did, they ignored it.

Reba took a swig of wine and looked me in the eye. "I knew all about them."

"Who?" I asked.

"That Sherman Stier and Shanna. I had a suspicion they were involved with each other. I have a lot of secrets that I know about a lot of people."

Pastor Tom put a finger to his lips to shush Reba. "Reba, dear, we've talked about this. The Lord doesn't like idle gossip."

Reba dismissed him with a wave of her hand. "Pfft. This isn't idle gossip, Pastor, this is active gossip. There's a big difference."

The pastor looked taken aback, and I could tell Bozeman was on the verge of laughter, so I elbowed him in the ribs to squelch it.

Reba took a drink, then continued. "They thought they were being sly, but I always have my ear to the ground, always. I learned they met up in Taos, where Sherman is from. Shanna met him at some bar up there, and he got smitten with her pretty looks and whatnot. Next thing you please, they were living together. I guessed right away that wouldn't work out. Shanna's too possessive, and Sherman is… was too much in love with money to be fully in love with her. That's why she moved back here."

Dean turned to Sam. "Did you know any of this?"

Sam shook her head no and was about to answer when Reba spoke up.

"Don't interrupt. I'm telling the story. Anyway, when he showed up in Quincey, Shanna assumed, incorrectly, that Sherman was interested in her. What he was really interested in was growing his fortune. Sure, they casually saw each other a few times, but he wanted nothing more from her."

"Bah, that's probably just a rumor," Rob said.

Reba pointed a finger at him. "Rumor my butt. Why, they came and stayed at my place one night. Shanna booked it with all the fancy sides I have. Wine, cheese, flowers, bubble bath, the works. I think that was her attempt to woo him back."

I leaned over and whispered to Bozeman. "Do people really woo? I thought that was just in the movies."

He shrugged.

Reba continued. "And although he had carnal relations with her that night, he didn't want her for forever, so she got furious at him." Reba took another drink and settled back in her seat, the story over.

"Love and money, the two biggest motives for murder," I said. "Pastor Tom, was that the big secret that Sherman came to you with? That he had that lurid affair with Shanna?"

I put the pastor on the spot. He tugged at his shirt collar and glanced around the table, only to notice that every pair of eyes focused on him. "I can't say, of course, I can't break the rules of confession. That would go against doctrine. I'm surprised you would even ask me that."

"My apologies, Pastor Tom."

Pastor Tom noticed he wasn't the center of attention anymore and threw me a quick wink. I smiled back at him.

"Anyone hear why Mayor Mary didn't show up tonight? Was she not invited?" Sam asked.

Lisa brushed away some crumbs on the tablecloth before her. "I invited her. I called her myself. She asked who else would be here, and the second I got to Dean's name, she politely declined the invitation, then rudely hung up on me without another word said."

It was Dean's turn to be the center of attention. "Well, what a few of you may not have heard is that our good mayor did some… inappropriate things on behalf of the town when dealing with the resort. Since those things have come to the surface, I think she's having second thoughts about being mayor."

I was curious, so I asked. "Are you still going to run for the job, Dean?"

Dean looked at me. "Yes. I still believe I can make a difference in Quincey."

"What about the future of the resort?" I asked.

"Well, from what I understand, Sherman was only the point person on that project, so whoever steps in to fill his position will probably carry it through. Although Stier, and to some extent, the mayor, went about things the wrong way, I think we all agree here that the resort would be a boon to this community. If, I mean when, I'm elected, I'll work with whoever's on that board to make sure that we meet the town's interests before those of the resort."

Rob raised his glass. "Here, here."

I glanced across the table at Sam. "Speaking of filling positions, I imagine you'll need someone new at the bakery."

"Why, Codi Cassidy, are you saying you'd like to give up that life as a country star to settle down and become a baker?"

I shook my head immediately. "No way. I wouldn't do it even if you paid me with blueberry muffins. That's a hard pass."

Lisa dropped her napkin on the table and stood up. "Actually, I might help you out there." She went through the swinging door into the kitchen and returned a few minutes later, dragging a young woman by the arm.

"This is Heather. She's my niece and she's come to stay with us for a few months. She's a hard worker, no, an excellent worker, and I think she'd be a great fit for your bakery."

Rob put a hand to his face so fast, he inadvertently slapped himself.

Sam noticed, along with the rest of us. "Do you have something to add, Rob?"

Rob shook his head, but Heather stepped forward. "Well, Rob's a nice man, and what he won't tell you is that I'm a walking disaster. I take orders wrong, I'm clumsy, and I spilled an entire bowl of soup on someone's lap yesterday."

Reba perked up at that news. "Who was it?"

Rob's face turned a shade of red. "Paul Peterson."

Reba laughed so hard her laughs turned to coughs, and when she took a swig of wine, it must have gone down the wrong pipe because she coughed even harder. I thought she might have a coronary, but she took a few sips of actual water and calmed down. "I can just see it, that pompous Paul Peterson with a lap full of… what type of soup was it?"

Heather glanced at the ceiling. "Tomato bisque."

Reba chuckled. "That's perfect."

Lisa broke in. "Oh, come on, dear, give yourself more credit. You're polite, and you're a quick learner. Maybe you're just not made to work in a diner. Not everyone is. Sam, what do you think?"

Sam looked Heather up and down. "Do you have any cooking experience?"

Heather shook her head.

"Have you taken any classes? Ever baked anything outside of a batch of brownies at home?" Sam asked.

Again, Heather motioned to the negative.

Sam paused, and we were all silent, waiting for the response. In the end, Sam smiled. "You know, I'm a sucker for hard-luck cases. Be at the bakery at six tomorrow morning, and we'll get started, okay?"

***

The next morning, I stepped off the bus at just after seven with bowls of food for the kids when I saw Sam walking across the lot, wearing her white apron and a wide grin. She was carrying a large box, and I hoped it was full of blueberry muffins.

"Here's a treat for the road. Thanks again for everything."

I called for Bozeman, and when he stuck his head out, I handed him the box. I nodded toward the bakery. "Did Heather show up at six?"

"No. She showed up fifteen minutes early. From what I've seen so far, it'll take her a bit to get going, but I think I can turn her into a baker."

We hugged.

"I'm going to miss you. The town will be quiet and boring without you here," Sam said.

"And I'm sure that's the way y'all will prefer it. Nice and quiet."

A tear formed in Sam's eye. "I owe you so much, you know."

I waved it off. "No, you don't. You carry no debt with me."

"When are you leaving?"

"Another hour. I need to feed Merle and Dolly, and Bozeman likes to give the bus a once over before we travel."

"Where are you headed next?"

"California."

"I hear there's gold there."

I shrugged. "We'll see."

I thought Sam was going to hug me again, but she didn't. She kissed my cheek, turned, and walked back to the bakery. I felt happy for her, and I was proud of her for showing such strength over the last few days. Someday, I hope to be strong like her.

I got back to work. I fed Merle, Dolly, Waylon, and Willie, then I cleaned out Dolly's stash for the day. It must have been rough scavenging because all she had under her blanket was a single shiny paper clip. I gave everyone some scratches, and ensured everyone was ready to travel, and then I double checked the area around the bus to make sure we would leave no trace.

Bozeman was ready to go when I buckled myself into the passenger seat.

"Ready?" he asked as he turned the key in the ignition.

I nodded. "Let's go. Time for our next adventure."

ABOUT THE AUTHOR

Dan DeKoning was born and raised in Milwaukee, Wisconsin, and currently lives in Knoxville, Tennessee with his wife and their cats.

He is a storyteller and poet who loves to write in a variety of genres and themes. He is also a voracious reader who loves to read anything he can get his hands on.

When he's not writing, you can find him hunting for treasures in used bookstores, or out exploring the planet, or geocaching, or searching for adventures and stories to tell.

ALSO BY DAN DEKONING

This is Dan DeKoning's complete library at the time of publication, but Dan has new books coming out all the time. Sign up for his newsletter at DanDeKoning.com to stay up to date on new releases.

<u>Fiction</u>
Déjà Vu
The Haunting of Hyacinth House
How Deep the Darkness

<u>Geocaching Mystery Series</u>
The Cacheland Conspiracy
The Quincy Bay Quandary
The Secret of the Seven Valleys
The Geocaching Mystery Omnibus – Volume 1

<u>Codi Cassidy Cozy Mystery Series</u>
Acoustics and Alibis
Ballads and Bloodshed
Codas and Calibers
Codi Cassidy Cozy Omnibus – Volume 1

<u>Poetry Collections</u>
Lost and Found
Random Thoughts